GW00391203

Steve McHugh

Hunted

Also By Steve McHugh

The Hellequin Chronicles

Crimes Against Magic
Born of Hatred
With Silent Screams
Prison of Hope
Lies Ripped Open
Promise of Wrath
Scorched Shadows
Infamous Reign

The Avalon Chronicles

A Glimmer of Hope
A Flicker of Steel
A Thunder of War

HUNTED

An Avalon Novella

Steve McHugh

Steve McHugh

This is a work of fiction. Names, characters, organizations, places, events, and incidents are either products of the author's imagination or are used fictitiously. Any resemblance to actual persons, living or dead, or actual events is purely coincidental.

Text copyright © 2019 by Steve McHugh

All rights reserved.

No part of this book may be reproduced, or stored in a retrieval system, or transmitted in any form or by any means, electronic, mechanical, photocopying, recording, or otherwise, without express written permission of the publisher.
Published by Hidden Realms Publishing

Cover illustration by Pen Astridge

To everyone who told me I needed to write a Remy story. This is for you.

CHAPTER 1

North Dakota, USA.

"You want me to jump off this cliff onto those rocks below?"

I was several hundred feet above ground, the forest stretched vast and unblemished before me. Directly below, a maw of jagged rocks awaited. I turned to Chao Wei, who stood twenty feet behind me, looking smug.

She nodded.

I glanced over the edge of the cliff then back to Wei. "Bollocks to that." Being British has always given me access to the best swear words.

As I headed back over, irritation radiated from her. "How long have we been here?" she asked.

"A month."

"How long have you been in your human form?"

"Nearly a month," I replied.

"We arrived and almost day one, you learned you could become human. Since then, you have spent your entire time here getting as drunk as possible and having sex with anyone stupid enough to agree to have sex with you."

"Yes," I said. "Yes, I have. Because, and I'm not sure if you're aware, but I was a fox for *hundreds of years!* Not a lot of humans want to have sex with fox-men, and those who do are usually people I want to run away from. I'm making up for lost time."

"You are dwelling in self-pity," Wei snapped. "Your friend died. I am sorry for that."

"Nate was murdered," I snapped back. "By Arthur, who was meant to be the good guy. Avalon have pretty much taken over the world, and we had to come to the arse end of nowhere just to stay ahead of them."

"You agreed to let me train you, Remy," Wei said, slightly kinder now. "But you have to actually trust me."

"By jumping off a four-hundred-foot cliff?"

"In your human form, you're all but impervious to harm. Your body heals almost instantly. You need to know the limits of that power. And if you die, you have plenty of lives left to come back," Wei said, slightly colder than I expected.

I sighed. She was, oddly enough, right. The coven who had cursed me all those centuries ago had done me that favor. Not by turning me in a fox-man hybrid—although I could think of worse things—but by dying in the process and giving me their souls. Twelve lives I had. I'd used five. Didn't mean I wanted to waste one of them jumping off a *fucking* cliff.

I returned to the cliff's edge. "If I do this, and survive, does that mean I get to continue to stay in my human form and not have you complain about it?"

"Probably," Wei whispered in my ear, before shoving me off the cliff.

I learned a few things falling off that cliff. One: I cannot fly by flapping my arms, no matter how hard. Two: four hundred feet rushes up on you pretty damn fast. And finally: rocks hurt like an absolute motherfucker.

The pain was total. It was an explosion of agony the likes of which I'd never felt before. My brain couldn't even comprehend what had been done to me, all it knew was to send a signal to tell me that every part of me hurt for what felt like a lifetime, and then the pain was gone. I stood on shaky legs; my very human body still knitting itself together. There was a large, ragged hole in my thigh, and a massive amount of blood splattered over the rocks that really should have still been inside me. But I wasn't dead.

I staggered to a nearby stream and cupped handfuls of cold

water, throwing it into my face. Blood stained the water that dropped back into the stream. What little of my clothes that remained intact, were also blood-spattered. I looked like something out of a zombie film.

"How are you feeling?" Wei called as she walked down the trail toward me.

"Like a fucking peach," I snapped.

"You look like a horror movie," she said with a smile.

"I can't go back into town covered in blood and with ripped clothes," I said, looking down at myself. "I only have one shoe."

"The other one flew off before you hit the ground," Wei said, putting a hand over her mouth as if trying to stop herself from laughing. "It was like watching Wiley Coyote."

"You pushed me off a cliff." I hoped my voice sounded angrier out loud than it did in my head. Honestly, I was just glad I'd survived.

"I told you you'd live," Wei pointed out. "You are not quite a *huli jing*, like me, but you're close."

The huli jing—the nine-tailed fox. Like me, they can turn themselves from human to fox. Unlike me they're still vulnerable in their human state. They're a rare species who use poison as their weapon of choice, have a dangerous talent for making people forget things, and just generally like screwing around with their victims as much as possible. They can also sense movement in the environment around them for some distance. It comes in handy to not only hunt, but also keep one step ahead of anyone hunting them.

Apparently, my powers in human form extend to not dying. Which is nice and all, but not feeling pain would have been helpful too.

"You could change back to your fox form," Wei suggested. "Then I would be convinced you were able to swap between forms easily, and I wouldn't have to see just how much punishment your human form can take."

My fox-man form was faster, stronger, and generally just all-around enhanced.

"You did this on purpose," I said. She knew full well the time and effort it took to switch between forms; knew, too, my super-healing only occurred in human form. "To make me turn back into a fox."

"Me?" Wei asked, brows arched with complete innocence. "I would never do such a thing. Also, yes, I totally did that. Human Remy Roax is, quite frankly, a bit of a dick."

That stung more than I expected. "Human Remy Roax—" Talking about yourself in the third person is the very definition of being a dick. "Human *me* is not a dick, I'm just trying to find my place."

"You know your place," Wei said, any trace of humor and mocking gone. Wei was hard to read at the best of times, and just when I thought I had a handle on her, she would flick a switch and change. It made getting to know her an extremely difficult proposition, which I got the feeling was exactly how she liked it.

"You are a warrior," Wei continued. "A great friend to many. And you make me, and many others, smile. Human you thinks of nothing but your own gratification. I understand they are the same you, before you start to make a snide comment, but you have to admit those two sides aren't matching up. You're like one of those idiots who does a whole month of remaining sober, and then the first day of being allowed to drink, you get so hammered you punch a police horse."

I knew she was right. Not about the police horse bit, that was weird. But I knew I'd overdone it. I'd been living to excess this last month. It wasn't just about being able to actually have sex as a human again, it was the need to actually feel something more than the rage and pain at what had happened to me and my friends. The fact my body healed itself so damn quickly meant I had to find quicker ways to get high or drunk.

"I'm going to go back to town," I said. "I'm hoping you have a change of clothes in your truck for me."

"I will give you clean clothes," Wei said with a frustrated sigh. "But then our time is done. You need to discover who you are and, frankly, I don't want to watch you self-destruct. I'll be staying at the cabin for a few weeks. If you decide you're done fucking and drinking yourself into an early grave, please come find me." She ran both hands through her long, dark hair and linked her fingers around the back of her neck, one of the few signs I'd been able to figure out—she was upset with me.

I didn't bother making a snide comment about how I'd just knitted my shattered body back together. I wanted to believe it was due to some deep personal growth, but frankly I was pretty sure Wei would just kill me then let me heal.

"If I die, do I keep the same powers I have now?" I asked as we walked back to her battered old Ford truck she'd picked up from who knew where.

"How long have you wanted to ask me that?" Wei removed a bag from the back of the truck and tossed it to me.

"From the moment I figured out what I am." I unzipped the dark green duffle bag and removed clean clothes. There was no use going elsewhere to change, Wei had chastised me for doing so the first time, and I didn't need to hear it again.

"Honestly? No, probably not," Wei said, any trace of irritation gone from her voice. "My guess is—and I'm trying to find evidence to back it up—every time you die, your powers reset. I don't even know if you'd be able to turn into a human, or if you can that you'd be the same as you are now. It's why we're here."

"So you can run experiments on me?"

Wei sighed. "Not exclusively, no. I agreed to help you because I like you, but I have to admit you have abilities I find endlessly interesting. Eventually someone will find you here, Remy. You have too many enemies for them not to. And when that happens, we'll have to move on. We do not have infinite time, not even here, in the middle of nowhere."

I looked at the expansive beauty that was North Dakota, a place we chose simply because of the lack of people here. A lack of people meant that, hopefully, it would be a long time before Avalon showed up and did what Avalon apparently do best—kill everyone.

It was my turn to sigh. "I worked for Avalon for a long time.

I didn't know that it was just a placeholder for when Arthur woke and took it all to the dark side."

"I actually understood that reference," Wei said. She'd spent a lot of the last half-century in the middle of Siberia, avoiding contact with as many people as possible. As a result, she didn't always get pop culture references, although for the last few weeks, she'd been educating herself during her time not spent torturing me.

"Well done," I said with an enthusiastic thumbs up.

"I can never tell when you're mocking me."

"Not this time," I assured her. As much as I had a hard time reading Wei, sometimes I got the impression the feeling was mutual. "Avalon are now bad. Very bad. And we don't have time for me to work through my issues. That's about the size of it, yes?"

Wei crossed her arms, a frown touching her features. "You don't sound like you agree."

"I'm dealing in my own way."

"Your way is wrong," Wei told me. "Actually, that undersells just how wrong your way is. Your way is stupid and wrong. And it will get you in trouble. Trouble we can ill afford."

"I'm pretty sure I can take care of myself," I told her. "But I'm also sure that my evening activities won't come back to bite us on the arse."

Wei stared at me for several seconds. "You know that it will now come back and bite you on the ass, yes?"

I nodded slowly. Sometimes my mouth is several seconds ahead of my brain. "I'm going back to town. I'm going to have a drink. Singular. And then I'm going to get my head in the game and come back here tomorrow morning for more torture."

"It's all I ask," Wei said with a beaming smile.

She climbed into her truck and started the engine. "You want a lift back to town?"

I knew how much she hated being near anything considered habitation, so I shook my head. "It's a half hour run from here."

"There are grizzlies around here, be careful."

"You just threw me off a cliff."

"Pushed," she corrected.

"You just *pushed* me off a cliff," I said. "Which is clearly much better than being thrown."

"We can try throwing next time."

"You know, with anyone else I'd think you were joking, but I'm pretty sure you're not."

"Watch out for bears, Remy."

I waved Wei off before turning toward the large woodland that separated me from civilization. Or at least as much civilization as this part of the world offered. The town of Hood, in the northern part of the state, had a population of just over four thousand; situated not too far from Devil's Lake, and few hours' drive from Bismarck, the state capital. Although, based on the lack of anything around Hood, it may as well be on another planet.

It was a nice town, with a few bars, some diners, and a sheriff's station that consisted of a dozen people. If Avalon did decide to come here and remove the inhabitants to get to me, there would be little anyone could do to stop them. Besides, I doubted I was anywhere near the top of Avalon's list, but it paid to be cautious.

It was a nice gentle jog back to Hood, and not once did I see a bear, although I did see a couple of deer. On the outskirts of Hood, I came across two red foxes and watched them scamper around for a few seconds before they stopped to stare at me.

"Is this the universe's way of telling me what I need to do?" I asked, and the two foxes darted off into the woods.

I entered the outskirts of Hood and headed down the main road to the bar where I'd rented a room. Despite being directly above one of the few bars in town, it was quiet. Even on the rowdiest of nights, I barely even noticed the noise. Although, I had to admit that I'd been down in the bar making the noise more often than not.

Several trucks were parked outside, and I avoided them all, walking around to the back of the three-story red-brick building, using the side entrance to access the stairwell to my room on the third floor. My room was of a good size, with bed, separate bathroom and kitchen, and a window that gave me a lovely view of the scenery to the south of town, where nature stood defiant against the half-assed attempt at whatever had passed for progress in Hood.

I ran a shower, letting the hot water remove the last vestiges of my blood, staying in until the water changed from pink to running clear. Only then did I get out, dry and dress in a dark pair of trousers, light green shirt, and charcoal waistcoat, keeping my dark green trainers as I hadn't been able to find a pair of shoes I'd liked. It was nice to wear something a little smart; it had been several hundred years since I'd worn anything close to as decadent as what I'd purchased in the last month. As a fox, leather armor was pretty much all I'd ever needed.

Studying myself in the mirror, I tied my long brown hair back into a ponytail. I wasn't entirely sure I should cut it, but there was always time for that later. It was just nice to feel... human. My yellow and black eyes looked like those belonging a red fox, there was no getting around that. I couldn't stay human forever. Nor did I particularly want to. I needed to help my friends. I needed to stop more innocent people being killed. But for now, I'd earned a break. Some time to reflect on all the horrific stuff I'd seen, I'd been through the last few centuries.

I grabbed a few hundred dollars from my wallet, putting them in my pocket. The bank card was too easy to trace, and seeing as I had several thousand dollars in a small bag hidden beneath the floorboard under my bed, I didn't need to use the card.

"One drink," I said to my reflection. "One drink. No fighting. No fucking. And then tomorrow we work properly." I sighed, dropping my gaze to the bare floor. "I miss you," I whispered. "Why'd you have to go and get killed, you stupid bastard?"

I glanced at myself in the mirror once again before staring up at the ceiling. "If there's a heaven, Nate, I'll see you there. And if there isn't... well, if there isn't, it was a pleasure to have known you."

I sniffed, taking a handkerchief from my pocket. "Damn it,"

I muttered, wiping my eyes. "Damn the whole fucking lot of it."

Nate would want me to fight back, to be the best I could be. If he were alive, he'd have been the one to shove me off the damn cliff. Or at least wet himself laughing when he saw me flapping my arms. But he'd have also been the first one at the bottom to help me should I need it. He sacrificed everything to give his friends a chance to defeat Avalon. It was a chance I aimed to take.

One drink.

Even I didn't believe that lie.

CHAPTER 2

I was only on drink two—whiskey neat—when I'd decided to sit at the bar because I wasn't sure how many times I wanted to walk over. I'd knocked the first one back in seconds, gaining a raised eyebrow from the bartender—a young man by the name of Danny.

"Remy, some people were in here looking for you earlier," Danny said once the bar area began to filter out as patrons received their drinks and walked away to whatever corner they'd decided to call home for the night.

Danny was a nice kid. He was also human, and with very little love for Avalon despite the news basically falling over themselves to wank off every Avalon employee they could get on their show. Danny had been working at a large newspaper in New York when the whole Avalon thing blew up, and told me very few people currently working there weren't paid stooges. Avalon had a lot of fingers in a lot of pies—journalism, politics, law, and probably more I couldn't think of. If humanity was to overthrow their invisible shackles, they'd have to start searching out information for themselves and not just switching on the TV to be spoon-fed what Avalon wanted them to believe.

So many of the non-mainstream sites were openly promoting insanity. I'd read one that suggested the enemies of Avalon were putting magic into the water that turned people into frogs. People believed this shit. Either out of ignorance, stupidity, or... actually, scrap that, it was almost certainly stupidity.

"So, these people…?"

"A man and woman," Danny said. "Both black. No names, just looking for a Remy."

"How mysterious," I said with a smile. "You tell them anything?"

"Told them to come back tonight and you might be here. They didn't seem like much of a threat. Both young, maybe early twenties, both looked a little scared if I'm honest."

"Okay," I said slowly, trawling through my memories to see if I could pick anyone out. "Anyone else?"

Danny nodded. "Grant and Dalton Anderson."

"Don't know them," I said. "Am I meant to?"

Danny leaned his elbows on the bar. "They're bad news, Remy. Grant is someone who likes to talk with his fists. It's rumored his wife was on the other end of that. It's also rumored that he sleeps around and is, frankly, a huge creep."

"Sounds delightful," I said. "And Dalton? Wait, isn't Dalton who Patrick Swayze played in *Roadhouse*? That's a real name?"

"What's Roadhouse?" Danny asked.

I stared at him for several seconds. "Fucking youth of today," I muttered.

Danny laughed. "Of course I know what *Roadhouse* is. Jeez, Remy, I don't live on Mars. Anyway, Dalton is at college on some wrestling scholarship. He's a dick. He was a few years younger than me at high school, but he was a bully and maybe got into a few nasty things with some drug dealers."

"So, they're both awesome people," I said. "Why would either of them want to speak to me?"

Dalton shook his head. "You don't remember?"

I shrugged. "Maybe. What am I meant to be remembering?"

"Remy Roax," someone bellowed from the entrance to the bar.

"Oh, shit," Danny said. "Do *not* start a fight in here. My boss will kill me."

I crossed my heart, and Danny rolled his eyes before turning to the newcomers. "Gentlemen, what can I get you?"

"Fuck you," the older of the two men snapped. "We want a word with him."

I looked at the finger pointed at me, and then beyond it to the short man it belonged to. He was balding, although trying to stave it off by having his hair cut short to his head. He'd been muscular once, and I could still see it in his arms and chest, although I didn't know if the pronounced belly was due to food or beer. There were several tattoos on both arms, one proudly stating he'd been in the army. He was clean shaven and had a scar just above his lip that moved to his cheek. It was jagged, so I assumed maybe a bottle or glass. The man moved like someone who knew how to fight but was well past his prime, and walked like someone who was full of piss, vinegar, and more than a little confidence in himself.

The younger man at his side him had mean eyes. That was the first thing I noticed. Then the overly-muscular physique, the black vest, the gold chain that looked like rope, the skinny jeans, the boots that I would put money were steel-capped; everything sort of fell into place. He was a douchebag.

"Gentlemen," I said with a flourish. "How can I help you?"

"You're the English prick we're looking for," the older man —Grant—said.

"I am English," I said. "And I do indeed have a prick. As far as chat-up lines go, it's a weird one."

That took him aback. "I'm not here to flirt, I'm here to kick your teeth in."

"May I ask why?"

The two of them shared an uneasy glance. They'd come to fight, and I was asking questions, making no attempt to do anything but sit and nurse my whiskey.

"My wife and his girlfriend came to this establishment two days ago," Grant said.

"Do you have names?" I asked.

"Of course we have names, you son-of-a-bitch," Grant snapped.

"My mum is called Lily," Dalton said, cracking his knuckles.

"My woman is called…"

"Jenna," I finished for him. "Two lovely ladies who came in for a drink. Ah, now I know who you are."

I knocked back my whiskey. "You," I said, pointing at Grant. "Cheat on your wife with anyone you can. You hit on everyone, including Jenna, by the way, who said you were gross. However, not as gross as the fact that you fucked your son's girlfriend when they were in high school, I think her name was Taylor?"

Dalton spun on his dad. "You did *what?*"

"Don't believe this shit," Grant said, clearly flustered.

"Oh yeah, he shagged her a lot," I continued. "Also, your teacher, neighbor, and two people he works with. I really don't get the appeal, but it sounds like you don't really know how to take 'no' for an answer, so I'm wondering how many slept with you just to get rid of you."

Grant's face was a furious shade of red, and several bar patrons were now listening.

"Oh, and you've hit your wife twice in the last year," I said, feeling the flush of anger at the thought. "Lily *hated* you. I mean, really *hated* you. She wanted to run for a long time. Because while she hates you, she fears her son." My gaze flicked to Dalton. "And you, Dalton, are a twat of the highest order."

Dalton stepped forward, and Grant rested a hand on his arm, motioning to those watching.

"You gaslighted your girlfriend," I continued. "Jenna is scared of you. You've never hit her, but you've come close. You've threatened her. And then you had the audacity to make her think it was all her fault."

"Where are they?" Dalton growled.

"Gone," I said. "I don't know where. I gave them money and told them to leave and never come back."

"Jenna will have gone back to college," Dalton said. "Fuck." He grabbed a glass from a nearby table and threw it across the room where it shattered against the wall, raining shards onto the ground.

"They left us messages," Grant seethed. "And a video." His

rage was almost total now, so I figured I'd help push him over the top.

"Of us fucking, I assume?" I nodded. "It was glorious. It was their idea to film it. We had quite the night. Both of you were out," I said, and pointed at Grant. "You with some woman at work, and Dalton with... your drug friends, I assume. So, they got a few hours to let off steam. And let me tell you something, they had *a lot* of steam to let off."

Someone in the bar sniggered, followed by someone else trying not to laugh.

"Gentlemen, I understand that I did things to your women that made them make noises they'd never made before, but I assure you it was only because you're both fucking arseholes that I was ever given the opportunity. Now, you came here to fight, but before we go out back and do this, I want to make something very clear. I'm going to hurt you. Both of you. Badly. I want you to know this because it's your fault. You can take the absolute shit kicking I'm about to dish out and change your lives, or you can wallow in your own self-pity, but if you try to do anything to those two lovely women, I will ensure you spend the rest of your lives hooked up to machines that help you piss."

"Is that meant to scare us?" Dalton said with a sneer.

"After you," I said and motioned to the rear door, which both Grant and Dalton walked toward, moving past me without a word.

"I thought they were going to fight in here," Danny whispered.

"Too many people," I said. "Grant is angry but not stupid. Dalton is both angry and stupid, but his dad is here. You're going to want to call an ambulance. Don't let anyone come out, I don't need witnesses."

"I'll make sure," Danny said with a nod. "Those two have enough enemies in town that no one is going to mind all that much if they take a kicking."

I left Danny to make the call, and walked out of the bar without another word, although I did check to make sure no one followed. The last thing I needed was me on the internet. And I certainly didn't need the cops turning up to have a chat.

Both Dalton and Grant were waiting in the private rear parking lot. Dalton on my left, bounced from foot to foot, practicing some quick jabs like he was about to take part in an MMA bout. Grant stood on my right, just staring.

"I hope my wife was good," he said, "because it's the last pussy you're ever going to get with that pretty face of yours."

"You think I'm pretty?" I asked with a smile. "Thank you so much. I mean, I thought I was a bit haggard today, but you saying I'm pretty just warms the cockles of my heart." I placed both hands over my chest and beamed at him.

"That's not what I meant," Grant shouted, spittle flying.

"But that's how I'm taking it," I told him. "Look, let's get this done, I have whiskey to drink, and wives and girlfriends to fuck."

Grant moved first, coming in with a left jab designed to move me toward Dalton. I swatted it aside, stepped around him, catching him in the stomach with a quick punch as I put the man between me and his son.

Dalton growled, and for a moment I wondered if he was actually human. I pushed Grant back into Dalton and watched as the younger man shoved his father aside. Apparently, discovering your dad shagged your girlfriend was not something he could easily get over.

I was not the best fighter in the world, but I'd been trained by the best fighters in the world, and while some of it was hazy, enough stuck that I knew what I was doing. Dalton threw a right cross, which I blocked and jabbed him in the throat with my fingers. He fell to his knees, clutching his neck and I drove my knee into his face with a satisfying crunch.

Blood poured from Dalton's broken nose as he rolled around on the ground unsure which part of his body hurt more. I kicked him in the balls. When you have the opportunity, why not?

Grant charged like a bull. and I spun; my roundhouse kick

a perfectly vicious strike to his head. Not something I'd usually employ in a street fight, but Grant dropped like a bag of hammers, his knee smashing into his son's face.

Dalton had probably suffered enough, but I kicked him in the balls again just to make sure. Grant though, well, he was a different matter. I'm not one for needing to go fight a man as some ridiculous measure of revenge for his hurting an innocent woman, but I'd liked Lily, and her husband had made her life miserable since they were teenagers. She feared him. Feared he'd find her if she ran. Feared he'd hurt someone she spoke to when out and about. Feared she'd have nowhere to go, that no one would help.

I have a particular hatred for men who attack the defenseless. A hatred I could entirely thank my dad for. I'd been on the receiving end of that attack more than once as a child. My dad was long since dead, but the memory of what he'd done was easily dragged back front and center when I saw it happen to someone else.

I kicked Grant in the ribs, flipping him onto his back as a whimper escaped Dalton. His nose was all but ruined and judging from the color and swelling around his eye, I wouldn't have been surprised if his orbital bone had been broken.

Grant rolled onto his front, so I kicked him in the ribs again with everything I had. His cry let me know they'd been broken. He slumped to the ground; his breathing ragged.

I crouched beside him. "You hurt someone you were meant to love," I said. "You did it because you're a weak, pathetic man who needs to hurt others to believe he's strong." With one swift movement, I grabbed his arm and broke his wrist. His elbow I snapped a second later, dropping the arm as Grant howled.

"She filmed you hitting her," I whispered. "Did you know that?"

He flinched, and the look of realization behind the pain in his eyes told me that was entirely new information.

"She wanted to take it to the police but the sheriff here is a friend of yours I hear," I continued. "Friend or not, you deserve this. That's the arm you used to hit your wife. I doubt you'll be hitting anyone with it again."

I clamped my hand around the broken elbow and squeezed, eliciting another howl.

"Are you done hurting him?" A soft voice asked from behind me.

I turned to see a black man and woman stood a few feet away. They were both no older than late teens, but their expressionless faces as they looked down at the mess I'd created told me they'd seen violence before, that they were used to it. I felt a twinge of sadness for them at that point.

"I assume you're the other two Danny told me about," I said. Considering the number of black people I'd met in Hood could be counted on one hand, it was probably a good assumption to make, but it never hurts to check.

"Are you going to kill them both?" the girl asked.

The man was just over six feet tall, while the woman barely over five. The man's hair was cut short, almost bald but not quite while her curls hung to her shoulders.

"We need to talk to you," the man said. His tone suggested it wasn't a request, which automatically made the words fuck off form in my mind.

I removed Grant's phone from his pocket and dialed an ambulance—just in case Danny hadn't done so yet—scrubbing the phone of fingerprints and dropping it beside him when I was done. "If we need to do this again, it'll be worse," I told Grant. "This is about as good a warning as I'm capable of. Be better."

I left the man whimpering on the ground next to his semi-conscious son, although the young lady put him in the recovery position, which was probably good idea. Didn't want him dying... actually, that's not entirely true. Honestly, I didn't care, but I didn't want to be arrested for him dying.

"We need to talk," the man said again. "My name is Jamal Cooper, and this is my sister Monique."

"Let's go talk somewhere that isn't about to become crawling with people," I said.

"You are Remy Roax, yes?" Monique asked as we set off together.

"Your accent changed then," I said, noticing the slight French tinge to it.

She nodded. "We are from Paris."

"Any chance that two French people aren't interested in my past?" I asked as we walked up a nearby hill and took a seat on a bench that overlooked a small pond. It was deserted and would remain so until school ended and the kids came here to do whatever it was kids did in the twenty-first century.

"You both came a long way to find me," I said, looking between the two. "So, this is either an attempt to kill me, or get something from me. And I don't have an awful lot."

"We're not here to kill you, Mr. Roax," Jamal said. "We're here because we need your help."

"To do what?"

Jamal and Monique exchanged a glance. "There's a coven in North Dakota teaching extreme levels of magic. Blood magic. Dark magic. They are killing witches who won't join, and they have a stranglehold on the town on Hood."

"You're witches, I assume?" I asked, ready to leave.

Monique nodded. "We are the descendants of those who turned you into the person you are today."

"Ah, well, you can both fuck off then," I said, getting to my feet.

"Remy," Jamal said, shouting after me. "They are murdering people. Good people. Innocent people. Not all witches are the same. Surely you know that."

I stopped. I did know that. I was friends with witches. I'd fought alongside them. I'd watched them bleed as they helped people.

I turned back to the siblings and sighed. "Start from the beginning."

CHAPTER 3

"Before you crack on with your, I'm sure, massively interesting story," I said. "How'd you know I was here?"

Monique and Jamal shared another quick glance. "We didn't," Jamal said eventually. "Not until two days ago."

Silence fell and I motioned for them to get on with it. "Yeah, you're going to have to do better than that," I said. "I'm a kind, generous, handsome man, but my patience does have limits."

Monique tried to mask her smile by turning away.

"We searched for you a few years ago," Jamal said. "I had this notion to try to make amends for what was done to you. That I would try to explain that not all witches were like that, but I found out you worked for Avalon and wondered what would happen to my sister and me if I did." He shrugged. "So, I left it and stayed away."

"You're doing a bang-up job of staying away," I said before I could stop myself. "Sorry, go on."

"Then Arthur announced to the world Avalon was exactly what so many of us had feared it to be—an oppressive, authoritarian monster. News travelled that a group had fought against their attempted invasion of Shadow Falls. Including a fox."

"Probably not a lot of those about," I said. I looked around to make sure we were still alone.

"None," Monique said. "Well, one, I guess technically."

With a nod, Jamal continued. "I was put in contact with some people you know, specifically a woman by the name of Diana. She told us you'd come to Hood. Then it was just a matter of asking around. You've kept yourself quiet. Judging from what we've heard about you, that was unexpected."

I smiled and got to my feet, stretching. "That sounds like something Diana would do. I can be stealthy when I want to be. While this is all quite lovely, it doesn't really explain why you're actually *here.*"

"Those centuries ago, when you were turned into a fox. The spell used was to *just* turn you into a fox, there were meant to be no deaths."

"Except," I said, "they wanted to hand me to a hunt to be torn apart by dogs."

Jamal dropped his gaze to the ground. "We have changed since then."

I nodded and retook my seat on the bench. "I know. I don't blame any of you. None of you were even alive. Doesn't seem much point in holding a grudge against people who weren't born until hundreds of years after it happened."

"Maybe we should just explain why we're here," Monique said.

"You're hunting a dangerous witch who is killing other witches," I said catching the sight of several birds flying by. I wondered how long we could actually remain where we were before some local passed. "You told me already."

"It is not the whole issue," Monique said. "One of the many duties the coven undertakes is to keep track of various witches who would become an issue. People who are dangerous, either to themselves or others. Witches share information with other covens around the world. It's not an exact science, and some are less willing to help than others but it goes a long way to ensure we are safe from persecution. We are here hunting a witch and we need your help. Those are true. But he is not a normal witch."

"He's powerful?" I asked.

Both Jamal and Monique nodded.

"His name is Louis Bonne," Jamal said softly, as if he was concerned that just mentioning his name would bring him to us. "He was born just a few years before you. Before you left France and moved to England."

"Yes, well a lot of French lords were getting parts of them removed by crowds of angry people, and my dad was nothing if not someone who ran away when needed. Honestly, he probably saved the lives of his whole family by doing so, which made it possibly the only good thing he ever did." I paused. "Apart from dying horribly."

An uncomfortable silence sat between them.

"My dad was a mean, nasty, drunk prick," I said. "There, that clears that up. Let's move on. Why is Louis Bonne capable of being over two hundred years old? Witches are mortal and live only human-length lives."

"He found a way to extend it," Jamal said, shifting his gaze to the lake. "To use the life force from others to extend his own."

"Like what happened with me?" I asked.

"Exactly what happened with you," Monique said. "Except for the fox bit."

"He killed a bunch of witches and absorbed their life-force?" I asked.

"Yes," Jamal said.

"So," I said, tapping my fingers against my leg. "He saw that the witches who tried to turn me into a fox managed to screw up, and used their screw up to kill a bunch more witches?"

"Not exactly," Jamal said.

Now, I was getting irritated. "You remember when I told you that I was handsome but not very patient?" I asked, turning my head slightly and smiling. "What the fuck is going on?"

"He screwed with the spell that was used on you," Monique whispered. "We found some journals he'd written where he had mentioned he was going to take the opportunity to do away with those in charge so he could become the coven's leader, but it went wrong. And instead of killing everyone and giving him their power, it gave it to you. And you still didn't turn into a fox."

I sat and thought about that for a few seconds. I'd always considered that my being a fox was down to the incompetence of those trying to do the magic but to discover that it was more down to one of their own murdering them all was pretty funny. I started to chuckle.

"It's not funny," Monique said.

"It is a bit," I said. "They tried to have me murdered in a horrific way, and one of their own murdered them first. I'm okay with it."

"He killed forty-six people over the next decade," Jamal said. "Until he perfected the spell."

"Shit," I said softly. "How many spirits did he manage to absorb? And why stop there?"

"We know of six spirits," Monique said. "Six innocent people. He never completed the spell. He was arrested by the coven and tried before being jailed in the Paris coven's dungeon. He remained there until the Second World War, when he was released by Nazis and vanished."

"Why is he here?" I asked.

"He was captured again in 1953 in California," Jamal said. "He'd left his notes behind in Paris, and part of his punishment was to have any memory of the spell he's tried to create, erased from his mind. But he knew enough, and was trying to recreate the spell from what remained of his memory. Nineteen humans were murdered before he was caught."

"And where was he sent after that?" I asked.

"There's a coven in North Dakota," Monique said. "They have a prison facility underground near the north of the state. He was sent there, and we assumed all was safe. Until Avalon happened. And then we started hearing about how he's taken over the coven and began murdering people."

"Bit of a coincidence that the only person who had been successful with the same magic that made me, is in the same state as me," I said.

"We thought that too," Jamal said. "In fact, we assumed you were here to stop him."

"Never even met him," I said. "That I know of, anyway." The realization that Wei had manipulated me into coming to North Dakota dawned on me. I thought it had been a joint decision, but thinking back on it, she had made the suggestion first amongst a bunch of other destinations that were completely inappropriate due to danger, or proximity to large populations.

"How many have died?" I asked after the silence stretched too long. "And why only send two young witches?"

"We are twenty-seven," Jamal said. "Not young."

"I stand corrected."

"We know of at least ten dead," Monique said. "And only two of us, because our coven has all but scattered to the wind. We've tried contacting people to help, but there's no one to ask for help. It's why we contacted your friends. We'd hoped to at least be able to find someone who could aid us. Hood is going to fall to Louis' control. People are dying. He wants to recreate something that never existed."

"And that is?"

"An immortal witch," Jamal said. "A witch so powerful that the use of their magic does nothing to age them. Who can use magic with impunity?"

"A sorcerer?" I asked. "He wants to be a sorcerer."

"There are distinctions," Monique said. "Sorcerers have fixed rules. Elemental magic, Omega magic, Blood magic."

"I've seen magic first-hand," I assured her.

"A witch who does not need to worry about using their lifeforce to fuel their magic is not limited to *types* of magic. They could use water and fire magic; they could use curses of incredible power. Runes that cause destruction the likes of which even the Norse dwarves would have found difficult. If you have no limits then magic, *all magic,* is wide open to you."

"And even sorcerers get exhausted," I said.

"He could put an entire life into one spell," Jamal said. "The results would be catastrophic."

"You want my help to track and kill him?" I asked.

"We don't even know how many lives he has now," Monique

said.

"If Mordred were here, he'd almost certainly make a Mario Brothers joke," I said.

"Mordred, the person who murdered indiscriminately throughout the centuries?" Monique asked, disbelief raising the pitch in her voice.

"Yeah, same guy," I said, resting my arms on the back of the bench. "Only, not really the same guy. It's a long and somewhat complicated story, but the short of it is; he was evil, now he's not. But his brain is a bit weird. He hums songs from video games."

Jamal and Monique glanced at one another.

"Yes, that's pretty much the expression everyone has when they meet him for the first time," I said.

"Can we get his help?" Jamal asked.

"If we need it, we probably can," I said. "But Mordred and the rest of my friends are trying to stay clear of Avalon's attention while Arthur and his goons murder everyone who disagrees with them. I'd rather not involve them unless we absolutely have to."

"We may need to," Monique said getting up from the bench and looking up at the night sky. "When Louis escaped, a lot of prisoners went with him. Most were low-level witches who committed horrific crimes, or humans who committed crimes against witches. None were good people."

"How many?" I asked.

"There were approximately a hundred people in that prison," Jamal said. "Fifty witches from the coven worked in the prison, many of whom are not accounted for. There's a small town to the north of here, about two hours' drive, it's close to an old abandoned US Military site that Louis and his people have taken over. We've been up there. It was bad."

"How bad?" I asked, not entirely sure I wanted to know but knowing I probably should.

"The coven had over five hundred members. We stopped counting the dead at fifty. We couldn't get close enough to the town to judge better."

"They were witches who were killed?" I asked. "Are you

sure?"

"They were cleansed," Monique said.

I looked between the two of them. "I have no idea what you're talking about."

Monique sat back beside me, and took a deep breath, exhaling slowly as if using the time to gather her thoughts. "It started with a general from Ancient Greece," Monique said. "He was a witch, and he had some Norse dwarves, or elves, or someone who was beyond evil, devise a way to ensure witches on the opposing side knew what would happen should they be captured. He called it a 'cleansing'. Essentially, you tie a witch to a cross that has had runes carved into it. You... you then cut open the witch and use their... blood to draw the same runes on the person's skin." She sighed, and I saw that it was difficult for her to describe.

"Do you want me to finish?" Jamal asked.

Monique shook her head, determination to finish the tale had her hands clench. "You encircle the base of the cross with blood to seal the circle of power. You're essentially using the life force of the witch to kill them. They... burst into flames. It's not fire, though. It's like napalm. From what I hear those runes were used in a slightly different way to create the sorcerer's bands."

"It's not a quick death," Jamal said, placing a hand on his sister's shoulder. "Our aunt was taken by a group of blood-cult witches and murdered this way. They believe it to be a way to gain power through the pain and suffering of others."

"And that's what Louis is doing?" I asked, unable to decide if I was more furious or horrified at what I was hearing. That such a thing happened to anyone was the stuff of nightmares. Sometimes I hear about people for whom stabbing is too good. Louis was quickly fitting that description.

"We believe so," Monique said. "Or at least he's convinced his followers that's what he's doing."

"Lots of evil witches just murdering anyone who disagrees with them," I said. "I get why you'd want to stop that."

"The cleansing was made illegal over five centuries ago," Jamal said. "It is a horrific way to die. And a horrific way to kill."

"Any chance the people who killed your aunt and the people doing all of these are the same?" I asked.

Monique nodded. "We think they broke Louis out of the prison."

"Why?"

"Louis is a sort of celebrity to these people," Jamal said. "They see him as some kind of *Robin Hood* character, except he murders those who hold back the downtrodden."

"Reality and myth are rarely the same," I said.

"I think some of these people wouldn't much care either way," Monique said. "Our aunt was a librarian. She had access to the books with forbidden magics in them."

"I assume they were stolen, yes?"

Jamal and Monique nodded.

"So, this has been in the pipeline for a while." I got to my feet, pacing as my brain went to work. "Possibly, they used the crimes committed by Avalon to spring the witches. Avalon don't much care if a bunch of witches get murdered. They didn't even care about the witches that were working *with them*."

"Witches worked with Avalon to murder people?" Jamal asked, anger creeping into his voice.

I nodded. "An English coven. They're dead now. All of them. And those that aren't, probably don't have a long life-expectancy. Avalon aren't known for keeping loose ends."

"Can you help us?" Monique asked.

I sighed and nodded. Would I have rather run in the opposite direction? Sure, but I couldn't just leave them both to deal with whatever horseshit Louis and his people were about to bring down on those who opposed them. Also, I quite liked Hood. Not all of the people—some were dreadful—but Danny and a few others had been welcoming and friendly, and it was picturesque in its own way.

"Thank you," Jamal said, shaking my hand, and clamping his other hand on my shoulder. It was the first time I'd noticed the strength beneath his calm exterior.

Monique stood. "May I hug you?"

I nodded. "Sure, why not."

Her hair fell over my face, and I tried very hard not to smell it, because smelling stranger's hair is weird.

"So, what do we do first?" Monique said as she stepped back, genuine happiness lighting her face.

"I'll get Wei," I said. "And we'll go look at this town of dead people. I want to know what we're going up against, and frankly, I doubt either of you have ever had a lot to do with dead bodies. Unfortunately, they don't bother me so much anymore." I glanced between the two. "Have either of you got combat experience?"

Both shook their heads.

"I did kickboxing as a child," Monique said. "But I haven't been to war or anything."

"I was never one who liked to fight," Jamal said. "I will if I have to."

"I'm not expecting either of you to be brutal killers," I told them. "Honestly, if it comes down to it, don't fight. Run. Doing the things I've had to do in my life is not a road I recommend for anyone. But I do need to see that place. Hopefully we can figure out what we're up against. Meet me at the bar later, we'll head over."

"Thank you," Jamal said. "Your friend Diana said that you would help. She also said that you would swear a lot... and be furry."

"The human look is temporary," I assured him. "And if you hang around long enough, you'll get to hear me tell people to fuck off in a variety of different and interesting ways. It's part of the charm. Probably. I'm not sure I know anymore. Anyway, meet me later. We'll go see about killing your murderous bastard friend."

"And what if he has more than one life?" Monique said.

"Then I guess we get to use him as a way to figure out more and more interesting ways to kill him," I said with a smile. "I've never seen someone torn apart by trees, so that could be fun."

"What? How?" Jamal asked.

"Search for it online," I said, and pointed at him. "Also, you're welcome for any nightmares that follow."

"I think I may leave it then," Monique said.

"Wise choice," I told her. "I'll see you both tonight. Do not tell anyone about what we're doing. I don't want the wrong person to overhear the wrong piece of info and we arrive at this military base with a lot of pissed off murderous cockwombles waiting for us."

"Cockwomble?" Monique asked.

"The internet is your friend," I called over my shoulder as I headed back to town.

An ambulance was just leaving the bar as I arrived, and I glanced into the main area where Danny was talking to a deputy while other members of law enforcement chatted to the remaining patrons. It appeared most in the bar had run the first chance they'd gotten.

I jogged up to my room, wondering if anyone would be waiting for me. No one was. I slumped on my bed and wondered whether waiting around while the police questioned people was a good idea. I sighed. Probably. Not. Besides, I needed to talk to Wei about just how much she'd set me up to deal with whatever awful shit was going on in Hood.

I grabbed my jacket and opened the door to find two deputies.

"Bollocks."

"Sir?" One of them asked. They looked similar in height, but one was bald while the other had long dark hair. They were both white and one of them had a skull tattooed on the back of his hand.

"Nice ink," I said, pointing to the tattoo.

"We need to talk to you, sir," the non-tattooed deputy said.

"About what?"

"About the assault of two gentlemen at this property earlier today," he told me. "It would be better if we did this inside."

I pushed the door open and turned; a sharp pain shot through my neck.

My knees buckled.

Darkness claimed me.

CHAPTER 4

I woke several times in the back of a vehicle. A thick fog clouded my mind, and I could barely keep my eyes open, but I heard someone say, "not again," and then felt another jab in the neck and slipped back to the land of sleep.

The next time I woke, I was on an uncomfortable mattress in a cell. I rolled to my left and fell the foot to the cold, stone floor, cursing anyone who might be listening as I sat up and took in my surroundings.

It wasn't great.

The cell was twelve feet by twelve feet, give or take, with a steel-framed bed and mattress, although to call it such did a disservice to actual mattresses. It might as well have been made of cardboard. There was a toilet at the far corner of the room, and a sink next to it. A small window let in enough light to tell me the sun had risen, but the window was high up and barred. Shouting would have done little good apart from make me hoarse. Besides, better to wait until my captors came to me. No sense in letting them know I was awake.

I checked every inch of the cell. Stone, concrete, and metal were all I found. No obvious way out unless I could suddenly burn through solid steel. Sorcerers had it easy.

There was a jingle of keys in the cell's lock, and I quickly sat on the bed and waited to receive guests. The door squealed as it was pulled open, scraping against the floor, and three men stepped inside—the two deputies from earlier, and a third man I didn't know. He was tall with dark skin, and short greying hair. Several rings adorned his fingers, all of which looked expensive.

"Easy or hard?" he asked me in a Canadian accent.

"Easy would be nice," I told him. "But then, you've been pumping me full of what I assume is tranquillizer all day, so I guess it's all subjective."

"You kept waking up," the tattooed deputy said.

"Am I meant to apologize?" I asked him.

"You're going to come with us," the man with the rings said.

I stood and stretched. "Fuck you. Fuck all of you with a rusty fucking hammer."

The punch to the gut was fast and hard. It doubled me over just long enough for one of the deputies to tranq me again. I was getting really tired of being knocked out. At some point, I was going to have to find something sharp and stabby to ensure it stopped.

I woke up for what felt like the fiftieth time that day, my wrists tied to a wooden cross beneath a sky of purples and reds. My feet rested atop a chair; at least I wasn't taking the tension of my entire body with just my arms. My mind felt woozy. And I really wanted to punch someone.

There were dozens of buildings around me, all identical in color—grey concrete walls and green sloped roofs. All were single story, and most had the windows boarded up. I caught sight of a twenty-foot-tall security fence and check point that lead out of what was clearly some kind of military installation, presumably the same one Monique and Jamal had spoken of. Two guards stood duty, but as there was a small guard hut, there might have been more inside.

Several crosses were planted in the far corner of the compound, each with the charred remains of some unfortunate bastard attached to it. The cleansing. I couldn't say it looked like a good way to go out.

The man who'd punched me, and his two deputy friends, were joined by four more. Three women, two of whom appeared to guards, considering their military fatigues and semi-automatic rifles. The third was talking to a man I'd never seen before. The woman had pale skin, and hair that was almost silver. She was maybe five feet tall, and her muscular arms held several rune tattoos. I had no idea what, or who, she was but doubted it was anything good. She turned to me, and even with the distance, her brilliant blue eyes shone.

The man she was with was a few inches shy of six feet, with a brown bushy beard streaked with grey. He was muscular, too, the tattoos on his pale skin matching those of the woman. They shared the same eye color, and I wondered if they were related... or if I was hallucinating bright blue eyes in people.

I smiled at the man who had hit me. "This the hard way?"

The man shook his head. "The hard way would leave you in more pain. This is a sort of midway."

"I've had worse," I said. "So, you going to torture me now?"

The man shrugged. "Not up to me."

"Up to him?" I asked, trying to move my hands to point toward the bearded man. "Louis Bonne, I assume."

At the mention of his name, the bearded man turned to me. He wore an expensive-looking red silk shirt that was undone, showcasing abs you could probably grate cheese on. His dark trousers and black shoes suggested someone who didn't care how out of place he looked, he had to let everyone know he wore expensive clothing.

"Aren't you cold?" I asked him.

"What?"

"Cold?" I looked around. "It's cold. Your shirt is undone. I assume on purpose and you didn't just lose a button or something."

"What are you talking about?" the man who'd punched me asked.

"Just making conversation," I said. "So, you're Louis Bonne."

Louis nodded. "And I am not cold," he said. "I am a master of my body. Cold is something felt by the weak."

"You've mastered the ability to not feel cold?" I asked. "You know, you could just wear a coat, right? That seems like an easier way to do things."

"Why are you in North Dakota?"

"Sightseeing," I said. "I heard the oil fields are really quite beautiful this time of year."

Louis nodded and the man who'd hit me earlier, punched me in the stomach.

"Nice," I said through gritted teeth.

"Roy here is well versed in hurting people," Louis said. "His government trained him for a long time in the art."

"Must be very proud," I said as my healing kicked in.

He hit me again.

"You really like your job." I spat onto the ground.

"Why aren't you a fox?" the woman interjected. Her accent was Nordic, but I couldn't quite place the exact country.

"You two related?" I asked.

"Not by blood," the woman said. She placed a hand on my torso, just above my hips, and pain flared through me like someone had taken a blowtorch to my insides.

I bucked against the ropes that bound me to the wooden cross and screamed until she removed her hand. I sagged forward, sweat dripping off me. "Fucking hell," I said through the pain. "What the hell are you?"

"You've heard of blood magic, I assume."

"Blood magic. That's years of your life, right there," I told her.

"It matters little when you have lives to spare," she said. "I expected someone a little more… furry."

"I expected someone a little less batshit crazy," I said. "Guess we're both disappointed."

She took a step toward me, and I tensed for what was coming.

"Susan," Louis said firmly. "Let's not take his life."

Susan looked up at me, her eyes alight with hatred. "As you wish," she said, and walked away, pushing past Louis and into a nearby building.

"She's awesome," I said. "Love her."

"You are an irritating man," Louis said. "You will tell me how you managed to survive the spell."

I tried to shrug, but it's hard to do when tied to a cross. "No idea. You're the one who screwed with the spell so the witches all died. I assumed you'd know more than most."

Louis regarded me for a moment. "I will be the ultimate witch," he said.

I laughed. "The ultimate witch? Holy shit, that's a dreadful name. I guess if you paint your face up, you could go be a wrestler with a name like that. *Ultimate Witch,* holy shit, that's golden."

"I will go back to those who cast me aside," Louis snapped, his face red with fury, the veins in his neck popping. "Those who tried to stop my progress will die, and I will eradicate their memories. I will remove the stain of their families from existence. Those two simpletons who came for you will be the last of their coven by the time I'm done. All who stand before me and my people will be removed. The true power of the witch will be laid out for all to see!" He stopped short and took a moment to regain his composure, he still looked angry though, although I guessed that was because I'd touched a sore spot and made him blurt out his bullshit plan.

"Quick question," I said, noticing the look of concern on several of the faces of those before me. Louis' madness was not something they enjoyed seeing.

Louis glared.

I scanned the group of witches before me. "Which one of you put fifty pence in the dickhead?"

They frowned, exchanging confused glances.

"You know, like one of those old game machines you needed money to operate," I said. "Seriously, people. If I have to explain the insult, is it even an insult?"

Roy punched me in the stomach several times in quick succession.

"Not a fan of comedy, eh?" I eventually asked.

"This is difficult to watch," Louis said. "I assume from how quickly you recovered from the tranquilizer that you heal quickly."

"Not really," I told him. "I'm just lucky."

Louis clicked his fingers, and someone ran over with a small packet. "You should have died," the man spat. "That life force that exists in you should be *mine*, yet you were given that gift. I wanted to hunt you down and cut you apart over and over again for that. I wanted to rob you of the gift I'd unfortunately bestowed on you in the most horrific ways possible. But..." He smiled then, "all in good time. After seeing you in your human form, I want to know more."

"I'm here because you want to know something I can't possibly tell you."

"You're here because you are an anomaly," Louis snapped, his eyes wide with madness. "You should be *dead*. You should have *died*, yet you were turned into a fox-man hybrid and now, seemingly able to turn back to human." The smile he gave me was a loathsome thing. "I wonder what happens when your power is taken away? Do you stay human? Are you able to shift into other forms? These questions need to be answered."

"You have your spells," I said. "You can absorb spirits, you're essentially immortal."

"No," Louis shouted, spittle flying. He opened his mouth to say more but closed it with a snap. He took a deep breath, and visibly relaxed before saying anything else. "Something isn't quite working, and you're going to tell me how to fix it."

And now we get to the crux of the matter. "Spells not working right?" I asked with a slight sneer.

"It works just fine," Louis snapped. "I just..." he cleared his throat, glancing at his underlings before lifting his shoulders. "I want it to be perfect."

I started to laugh. "You can't remember how you perfected it last time, and you think I know," I said. "I'm just the dumb idiot who pissed off a witch, I don't know how to make your spells work."

Louis' face contorted in rage, and he snatched the contents of the packet free before striding over to me. He wrenched the chair and, stepping onto it, placed the sorcerer's band on my wrist.

"You will tell me," Louis said as my body immediately stopped being able to access whatever power I held.

I'd changed from human to fox and back again a few times, but never like this. My entire body felt like it was on fire, burning from the inside out, and I screamed in Louis' face as my bones broke and were remade in an instant. My muscles snapped then tore. My entire being screamed in pain as Louis stepped from the chair, a look of concern on his face. Had he just killed his hope to figure out what he'd done wrong? I had no idea because I was shrieking like a fucking banshee.

My limbs contorted, waves of agony pulling and tearing and shifting until it felt like my entire world consisted only of torment. My hands slipped through the bonds and I fell to the ground as rust-colored fur pushed like red-hot needles through my skin. Patches of yellow and white fur ringed my throat and led down to my stomach. I stood, all three-and-a-bit feet of me, radiating utter fucking hatred for the absolute bastard who had just put me through that torture.

The clothes I'd been wearing pooled around me, and I kicked off the trousers, but kept the shirt, even though I probably appeared quite ridiculous. I looked at my wrist and saw that the sorcerer's band had shrunk with me. *Bollocks.*

If I tried to force it open without the key it would ignite in magical napalm. I'd never heard of anyone surviving such a thing. I didn't really want to test it out.

Louis clapped and I wanted to punch him in the dick.

"You remain a fox," Louis said with a smug grin that made me want to tear his face off *and* punch him in the dick. "Interesting."

I breathed out slowly, feeling the pain fade, looking down at my almost fox paws. One of the best things about being a fox-man hybrid, apart from being generally awesome, is the opposable thumbs. My hands look closer to paws than anything a human has, but the thumbs really were a superb addition.

"You're murdering people," I said, my voice remaining the same whether human or fox. It freaks some people out first time they hear it. "Witches as well as humans. Are these people okay with that?"

"*My* people are okay with it," Louis said, turning to Roy. "Tell him why."

"Witches have been held back for too long," Roy said by rote. "We will rise up. And you are either with us, or against us. They were traitors to their kind and were treated accordingly."

"The witches who did this to me were assholes," I said. "They thought they had all the power, and believed they had the intelligence and duty to carry out my punishment as they felt fit. But they were just assholes. You're all fucking evil."

"It's only evil if you're on the other end," Louis said, still wearing that smug grin. "Those who win get to decide what is evil and what isn't."

"No," I snapped. "Evil is evil. Doesn't matter what side you're on, you're still shitheads."

"How black and white of you," Louis said with a snort of disgust.

I shook my head, my whiskers twitching in anger. "Not really. There are lines you don't cross. You don't murder innocent people, you just *don't*. All you care about is power. You crave it, you need it back, but you don't know your own spell," I said, my claws sinking into the dirt. "And you need *my* help to figure out how you got it to work last time. Well, I think I can say with heartfelt honesty, that you can go fuck yourself, you warped piece of dick cheese."

Louis' scent was full of rage and hate and little else. The scents of those witches around him were similar, but mixed with concern, fear, and a little bit of excitement. My tail twitched, and I rolled my shoulders acclimatizing myself to being a fox again. I considered making a run for it, but several of the witches aimed guns at me—presumably a measure to ensure I didn't run—and I wasn't sure I could make it to the woods before I got hit.

"Is that your final answer?" Louis asked, and even if his

scent hadn't been full of hate, I'd have been able to see it radiating off him like a solid wave.

"No," I said. "I'm going to burn you and your operation to the ground. Every *one* of you is going to die. Horribly. And when it's all done, when you're all smoldering sacks of shit on the ground, I'm going to piss on your ashes."

Roy kicked me in the ribs, punting me to the ground, where I remained until he closed the distance between us. Roy tried to grab me, but I was too quick and easily dodged aside, standing a few feet away and closer to the woods as Roy looked irritated that I'd... well, to be frank, outfoxed him.

Louis moved closer. He crouched in front of me, his face only inches from mine.

"I am going to have to cleanse you," Louis said. "I will just have to figure out my spell on my own. You are of no help."

He jabbed me in the nose with his finger. I moved faster than he expected, my needle-like teeth snapping through flesh and bone. He screamed as I spat his finger back into his face.

"Tastes like chicken," I said, before I turned and sprinted away toward the forest as medics we're called for Louis.

Gunfire followed me, dirt kicking up around me as I zig-zagged to the end of the compound away from where the most armed guards were. While the compound was in the middle of the forest, I didn't want to get shot trying to escape.

I scaled the fence in seconds, and as I swung myself over the barbed wire, I saw the fifty foot drop close to the edge that ended in a nearby stream. The sound of barking dogs ignited the fear at having to escape them without weapons. The water was my best hope. I let go, a stab of pain hitting just below my ribs as I fell.

I hit the ground hard, lost my footing and tumbled down the hill. Pain exploded at the back on my head, turning my world dark then the shock of freezing water had me gasp for breath. It was a lot more than a stream and the current had hold of me. I struggled to stay conscious as my arms and legs felt heavy, my tail dragging me down under the water as I fought for breath. Pain exploded in my chest, and I surrendered to the blackness, to the sounds of dogs barking in the distance.

CHAPTER 5

Whenever someone blacks out at sea or in a river in the movies, they always wake up on the bank or beach with few ill effects. Yeah, that didn't happen to me.

The shirt I'd been wearing was now entangled in a tree branch across the river. I was still in my fox form. The fast-flowing water was waist-deep, and I was numb. I looked back but couldn't see the hill from where I'd fallen. At a guess, I was pretty sure it had been a considerable distance. I took hold of the branch, and pulled myself along it to the bank, gut-wrenching pain coursing through my body with every movement.

I flopped onto the bank and steadied my breathing, trying to calm myself. I had a few problems that I could see. I was injured; my legs were still numb and until that went away, I couldn't get very far. Add exhaustion, my head hurt, pain in my gut, my tail was sore from a hit I didn't remember taking, and I still wore the sorcerer's band. Turning back to human to heal was impossible; removing the band would kill me, and that death might stick. It depended on whether my powers kicked in before I died. I couldn't kill myself and just have one of my other lives bring me back; I wasn't even sure that was possible with the band on. Essentially, I was fucked. And somewhere in the distance were witches with weapons and dogs with big teeth hunting me.

The sky was quickly moving to darkness, and I probably didn't have long before they were on me. I needed to get warm, and I needed to get moving. Not necessarily in that order. I tried to stand but my legs were still wobbly, so I dragged myself away from the river and slumped next to a large boulder.

My concern at the constant ache in my side rose when I spotted the bullet hole. It was a through-and-through, about a half inch from having missed me completely. I didn't think it had hit anything vital, and the blood wasn't gushing, which was helpful, but it still needed looking at. First, I needed to stop the bleeding, then I'd think about the possibility of infection. Best plan was to get to Wei's hut, but seeing how I had absolutely no idea where I was in relation to said hut, that was probably going to be an issue.

I scanned the dense forest; I'd heard a few people in Hood talk about coming out here to hunt, legally or otherwise. I pulled myself upright and my legs held with only a small tremble, although the pain that shot through my side and up my body caused me to cry out. Being shot sucks ass.

I sniffed the air. Closing my eyes and taking in long drags of scent to try and get a better picture of what was around me. Humans had been here recently. Their scents were mingled with animals, but humans being here meant they either lived nearby or had parked their vehicle and gone hunting. At least I hoped so, and seeing how hope was in short supply, it was what I was going on.

I'd torn the shirt free from the tree, but the remains of it were still draped around me like a giant tarpaulin, although it had been torn to shreds by the branch and was pretty much soaked. I tore it free, wrapped strips off it, using them as a tourniquet around my waist. It wasn't much, but when your options are bad or worse, you pick the one that keeps you alive the longest and deal with it when you can.

I stumbled through the forest, half on two feet, and half on four, never finding either to be pain-free for long, following the scents that crisscrossed one another. There were at least four men, and they'd gone to the river and doubled back into the forest. I wasn't entirely sure where I would end up, but anywhere not with people shooting at me was better than somewhere with them.

While I had to stop a few times to catch my breath, the scents eventually led me to a small hut that, judging from the dissipation of scents, had been empty for the better part of a day. The door was locked but I threw a rock through the window—opposable thumbs for the win— then used a branch to clear away the glass, and managed to climb in, causing more pain in the process.

The hut had two double bunks, a stove that was still warm to the touch, and a large first aid kit. I upended the kit, dropping a knife and various bandages and creams onto the floor. I picked up the knife. I didn't want to have to cauterize the wound. Not just because it hurts like fuck, but also because it's not quite the simple process films make it out to be, and you're more likely to pass out from pain than anything else. Also, it hurts like fuck.

As I was sorting through the kit, I noticed a duffle bag stashed under one of the bunks. It was heavy, and did little to help with the pain, but it held more first aid items. I grabbed some square sterile bandages, enough baby wipes to ensure the clean bottom of every baby in North America, and an unopened bottle of whiskey.

With whiskey and wipes I cleaned myself up, which is easier said than done when every touch is agony and you're covered in fur. Still, I managed it, and sat back panting after pouring more whiskey over the two bullet holes.

I cut away as much fur as I dared, which I added to the list of shitty things I'd had to do. The bleeding had slowed but the pain remained, so I added the sterile bandages, putting another two over the first set, and took several powerful pain killers chased down with whiskey. Pretty sure that the instructions advised against it, but I doubted it said how many to take when you've been shot, so fuck it.

Slumped on the ground, the darkness that had been threatening to take over pushed the last pieces of light from the sky. I wondered how long I had before Louis and his merry band of dickheads found me. I guessed I was some distance from the compound now, and hadn't heard or smelled any dogs since falling in the river. While I could see in darkness just fine, travelling through the forest on foot... or paw, at night was probably asking for trouble. I needed rest. I needed sleep. The clock on the wall indicated it wasn't particularly late, so I took a moment to close my eyes, telling myself that I was moving on soon.

In the end, my body decided for me and when I opened my eyes, four hours had passed. I ached and my side hurt, but no blood seeped through the bandages. Apparently, I'd done enough to at least not die immediately. Good to know.

Using the frame of the bed to pull myself to my feet, I was unsteady but I'd live. Just had to figure out exactly where I was and how to get to Wei's cabin, and I might be able to go back to that compound and murder every single bastard. Revenge is a hell of a motivator, especially when you've had the shit kicked out of you.

Somewhere in the distance, the rumble of an engine had me freeze. If I left the cabin and ran for the cover of the forest, I wasn't going to get very far before I was caught. I was stronger than a human, but humans and dogs would not make for fun adversaries.

I crouched as car lights shone through the broken window before the engine was switched off.

The lights remained on.

"Dad, look." It was a girl's voice. She sounded young.

"Looks like something took a liking to the hut," a man said. "I'll check, you stay back."

There was a noise, like the cocking of a gun, and then a key was put in a lock. I readied myself for a fight, but some instinct inside me said these people weren't those who had aided in my capture and wounding.

The door was pushed open and torchlight moved over me.

"It's a fox," the girl said from beside the man. She was no more than ten or eleven.

"I thought I told you to stay back," the man said, although there was little anger in his voice. And a serious amount of fear.

"Foxes don't stand on their back legs like that," the girl continued, looking down at the first aid contents spilled across the floor.

"Not quite a fox," I said, keeping my hands where they could see them.

The shotgun in the man's hands remained pointed away from me, and he showed little surprise at the fact I was speaking. "You one of those sorcerers?" he asked.

"Not so much," I said. "Can I lower my hands, I'm in quite a bit of pain here."

The man nodded. "You're hurt?"

It was my turn to nod. "Shot. Through and through. I've stopped the bleeding, but it needs looking at. My tail too, hurts like hell, but that's harder for me to check."

"What's that on your wrist?" the girl asked, taking a step into the cabin before the man stopped her.

"Sorcerers band," I told her. "Bad things devised by bad men to stop others from using their abilities."

"So, you're a were-fox?" the girl asked, her tone suggesting more wonder than I currently felt was necessary.

"No, just a poor idiot who got tangled up with witches a long time ago. Look, I didn't mean to cause you problems, I just needed somewhere safe to patch myself up." I looked between the girl and the man. "She your daughter?"

The man nodded, his eyes never leaving mine. He wasn't afraid anymore, and he wasn't angry, but he wasn't curious about me and apprehensive about my situation.

"If you have a phone, I can call my friend and get out of here," I said. "I don't mean you any harm."

"We saw the news about people like you," the man said. "They say that you're with Avalon or you're monsters who murder humans for sport. That true?"

I shook my head. "Avalon aren't exactly the good guys."

"And the people after you, they Avalon?"

I shrugged. "Not sure. They *are* bad people though. Witches. A coven who want to become more powerful than they currently are. They've been killing people in Hood."

"I know Hood," the man said. "Know the sheriff there is a

corrupt piece of shit."

"Dad," the girl almost shouted.

A smile creased the man's lips behind the beard. "We have a cabin a few miles from here, you coming in tripped some motion detectors I had put in. We had an issue with kids and then an issue with a bear, and then the issue sort of fixed itself."

"The bear ate them?" I asked.

"No, but I doubt they'll be coming back here any time soon." He looked behind him at the darkness of the forest. "Come with us, we'll take you to the cabin, get you seen to. I was an army medic, so I have some experience with patching up bullet wounds."

"It would be dangerous if these people find me," I said.

"And you'll be dead if you stay out here. You have no means of contact, no means of getting to your friend, and no means of stopping that wound which, by the way, is seeping through the bandages."

I looked down at the bright red spot on the bandage. It was growing.

"I'll make a call, and I'll be gone as soon as they come," I said. "If I can get this damn bracelet off, I can heal myself."

"Those things stop you from being able to heal?" the man asked.

I nodded.

"Mary, help the... I'm sorry, I don't know your name," the dad said.

"Remy," I told him. "Remy Roax."

"I'm Travis Brighton and this is my daughter Mary," Travis said.

"Nice to meet you both," I said, and let Mary help me out of the cabin and into the back of the truck.

Travis and Mary climbed into the front seats, with the latter turning back to me. "I've never spoken to a fox before."

"I'm not sure there are any more foxes that can talk," I told her as the car started and we moved away from the hut.

"These witches," Mary started, "why did they try to kill

you?"

"I don't think they were very happy with my reply to help their leader search for a way to hurt more people."

"You said no?" Mary asked.

"Something like that," I told her, and saw the smile on Travis' face in the rearview mirror.

Mary continued to talk to me the entire drive, presumably so that I didn't pass out. When we stopped, and both helped me out of the car, I found myself in a well-stocked garage.

"We have a bathroom with the things I'll need," Travis said. "It's small, but stocked, and I can look at your wounds. You can call your friends too." He turned to his daughter. "Get the phone."

"You went out at night without a phone?" I asked him.

"Didn't realize I didn't have it until we were almost there," Travis said when Mary went to do as she'd been asked. "If I'd told Mary, she'd have told her mum, and then I'd be hearing about it for a week. My wife, Hannah, she's Mary's mum, has rules. One of which is a cell at all times."

"Smart woman."

"My dad always told me to marry someone smarter than me," Travis said. "He was right."

"But she'd have still been mad at you for forgetting your phone."

Travis smiled again. "Yes, she would. And I'd deserve it too."

"What does she do?" I asked as Travis helped me up the short staircase and through a door that lead into a hallway.

"She's a doctor," he said. "A surgeon."

"So, you didn't just go smart, you went exceptional," I said as Travis opened a door to a small but well-kept bedroom. He removed a bright blue blanket from one the fitted wardrobes and placed it over the bed.

"Yes, sir, yes I did."

I sat on the bed as Mary returned.

"I'm going to go scrub up and see what we have here," Travis said. "Mary is going to go boil some water and get some towels."

Mary turned and ran out of the room.

"How are you so calm?" I asked him.

"Not calm," he said. "Just trained not to freak out." Travis followed his daughter a few seconds later, leaving me alone with the phone.

"Where are we exactly?" I called after them.

Travis told me the exact co-ordinates for the cabin, and I dialed Wei.

"And this would be?" she asked.

"It's Remy," I said softly. "I'm in trouble. I need your help."

"Remy?" Wei asked, and I heard the concern in her voice. "Tell me where you are. And then you can tell me what the hell is going on."

CHAPTER 6

"Thank you," I said to Travis as I handed him back his phone. "Wei said she'll be here within the hour."

"We still need to look at that wound," Travis said, placing a black leather bag on the floor.

"Do we really?" I asked. "Once this bastard thing is off, I'll be able to heal. Unfortunately, I need a key"

"Did your friend say she had a key?"

I shook my head. "No, she didn't."

"So, it could be a while."

I nodded. "It could be, yes." I sighed, resigned to what was to come.

Travis got me to lie down then removed the bandages from my side. "At first glance, this looks okay," he said. "Through and through, no serious damage to organs from where it's hit, but something is off."

"For the last few minutes I haven't been able to smell anything," I said. "That seems bad."

"Can you usually smell anything?"

"I'm still part fox, so yes. My sense of smell is excellent, better than most dogs. It's what I used to find your cabin, but I couldn't differentiate the scents. At the time, I thought it was just the shock of what had happened, but when you and Mary turned up, I could smell you both, smell your fear and apprehension. Smell Mary's excitement. Since then my sense of smell is lessening. I'm not sure it's shock." In all honestly, I was terrified it was something much more serious, and was one of the reasons I hadn't been keen on Travis looking at it. Getting the band off was the priority, but it probably wouldn't help much if I was dead before that happened.

"There's some kind of silver fluid leaking out of the holes," Travis said. "Looks like molten quicksilver."

I shrugged. "No idea," I said between clenched teeth. "Some kind of witch bullshit, I imagine." I'd been shot with a silver bullet before, I knew the pain it caused, and this wasn't like that. It was like a gradual shutting down of my senses. The sorcerer's band didn't do that, at least none I'd ever worn before had done that, and I'd seen people draw runes on bullets to cause extra suffering to their victims, so it wasn't outside of the realm of possibility.

"I need this *thing* off me, and I'll be fine," I said. "I just need to not die before then."

I felt a slight jab near the wound.

"Local anesthetic," Travis said. "Should stop this part from hurting too much."

"What part?" I asked.

"I have to clean this wound. It has bits of tree and dirt in it. And then I have to sew it. None of that is going to feel good."

"Lucky me," I said and took a deep breath. "I hope you have sterile tools."

Travis nodded. "I'm going to go wash up again, and then we'll get you done."

I remained motionless while Travis left the room, Mary remaining behind.

"It looks bad," she said.

"You do not have a great bedside manner," I told her with a smile.

"Will you be okay?"

I nodded. "Had worse."

"Really?"

Another nod. "I jumped off a cliff only a few hours ago. I

once had one of the Ancient Greek gods kill me. That wasn't fun."

"What happened to him?" She stopped. "Or her."

"His name was Helios," I said. "He's exceptionally dead."

"How can you be more than just dead?" she asked, tilting her head.

"Point taken. Let's just say that he died hard, and he deserved every second of it."

"Do you have any other animal friends?" Mary almost whispered. "Like a talking horse?"

I laughed, which hurt, and I nearly swore, which I was pretty sure would teach Mary some new and unwanted words, but I managed to keep it together. "No, sorry," I said as a tear ran down my cheek.

"What about talking rabbits?"

"No rabbits," I said. "I'm going to make this easy for you. There are no talking animals except me. And I guess weres, but they can't talk when in their animal form, so maybe just me."

"You're unique," Mary said.

"I am," I said as Travis re-entered the room. He'd donned surgical gloves and wore the expression of a man who was about to do something he really hadn't expected he'd be doing.

"Mary, can you go watch something on the tv for a while?" Travis asked his daughter. "I think you probably shouldn't be watching this."

"Okay, Daddy," she said, before turning to me. "You'll be fine. My dad saved his friend's life in the war."

I nodded. "I have no doubt."

Mary left, and Travis set to work the second he was sure we were alone. He'd brought me a piece of wood to bite down on, which was used more than once during the ordeal. It could have been worse, I guess. I could have been literally on fire. That would have been worse. Otherwise, even with the pain relief, it still hurt like an absolute bastard.

When it was over—which felt like a thousand years—I was drenched in sweat, and there was a stack of wipes next to me, along with a bowl of hot, and now bloody, water,

"I've stitched you up, and cleaned you out," Travis said. "Not in that order. That weird silvery substance looks like it belonged to the tip of a bullet. I think it melted once it hit you."

"Evil witch bullshit," I said, and sniffed the air. "I can smell. I think it was a rune-scribed bullet. Not silver but designed to screw you up once inside you. Thankfully, I'm small enough that it went right through. Doesn't hurt so badly now, either."

"You'll still need to get it looked at professionally, but you'll survive the night."

"I can't thank you enough," I said. "I'm sorry I brought my troubles to your door."

He gave me a nod. "I saw some pretty awful stuff on deployment, and I also saw a man turn into pure fire and fight another man who managed to conjure creatures of rock out of the ground. Turns out, I saw a fight between an elemental and a sorcerer and was lucky I wasn't killed in the process. I had a very long talk about what I'd seen, so while this has turned out to be a strange night, you are not the strangest thing I've ever witnessed."

The following laugher was something I immediately regretted. "And I'm sorry your daughter had to see me all bloody and banged up."

"She's a tough kid, she'll be fine. It's not like I could just leave you there."

"And your wife?"

"I'll tell her about it in the morning. She doesn't need to be woken just to tell her that everything is okay."

Mary appeared in the doorway. "I see lights outside."

Travis ran to the door, and I followed suit, although at a much more sedate pace. I trailed behind the pair as they moved through the cabin to the front windows. The cabin was enormous, certainly much larger than I'd first anticipated.

"Vehicles," Travis said. "Five, I think. Nope, six. Coming up the road toward us. I do not think they're here with good intentions."

"Let me get out there, lead them away from you," I said. "There's no need for you to do anything else today."

"If you go, will they ignore us and come after you?" Travis asked. "Will they believe me?"

"I don't even know how they found us," I said.

"We didn't rat you out," Travis said firmly as Mary ran over to the light switches and bathed us all in darkness.

Mary picked up the landline phone. "It's not working."

"I really am beginning to see why you hate these people," Travis said.

"I know," I told him. "More witch magic. I'm trying not to hate witches, but they're not exactly making it easy. You have weapons, I assume."

"My father-in-law paid for this cabin," Travis said. "He likes his guns, so yes, we have weapons."

"You should take Mary and run for it," I said.

"They'll get us before we're even halfway up the road to hear," Travis told me. "Besides, I have another idea."

The first of the cars pulled up out the front of the cabin and killed the engine. Four men climbed out, each with a rifle, although I couldn't say for certain what kinds they were.

"You got a tank?" I asked.

"Sorry, just guns," Travis said. "Mary, you can't stay in here."

"I'll go to the panic room," she said.

"You have a panic room?" I asked.

"My father-in-law is both rich and paranoid," Travis told me. "That's between us, Mary," Travis shouted after his daughter, who stopped on the stairs and gave the thumbs up.

"Is it safe?"

"It's bomb proof," Travis said. "She could live in there for a month."

"You should go with her," I said. "Hell, we both should go with her."

"Too much here leads to my address," Travis said with a shake of his head. "We go in there; they find out where I live. Not going to risk it. And I can hardly let you do this alone. You're still weak."

"And feeble," I said with a smile. "Maybe they'll be nice if I just tell them how sick I am."

I followed Travis into a room, where he typed a six-digit number into a keypad. He opened the door, and I let out an involuntary gasp. "That's a lot of weapons," I said. "Is your father-in-law planning on invading a country?"

The dozens of rifles sat on racks on the far wall; glass cases beneath contained pistols and revolvers. Swords and daggers were stored on the wall to my left, and on my right a hodgepodge of various muskets and revolvers that probably wouldn't have looked out of place in the Civil War. A dozen portable safes sat against the walls, each one with a keypad. Travis put the codes into two and opened them, revealing hundreds of rounds of ammunition.

He removed an 1887 Winchester rifle from the rack and passed it to me, grabbing a box of 10-gauge cartridges for it on the way. "You okay with this?"

I loaded five of the cartridges into the gun and took the remainder with me back into the front room, Travis close behind. He'd taken two Glock's although I couldn't tell which make, and two rifles. We both crouched near the large front windows and placed the guns between us.

"Timber Classic Marlin 336C," Travis said, picking up a leaver rifle. "I figured if you can use the Winchester, you can use this."

"And that one?" I asked, pointing to the black rifle Travis was currently loading with a magazine.

"Mauser M18," he said. "Five shots, hope we don't need them."

I peeked over the window ledge. "They're just waiting around."

The sun was just about to break, and the sky was cascading with color. Full daylight would come soon, and I doubted the witches wanted to wait for it. I spotted Roy, ordering his comrades about. I really wanted to shoot him, but I also wanted to see what they planned to do first.

"Getting you and Mary out of here is priority one," I said

and winced at the pain in my side. The pain relief was beginning to wear off.

"I have enough bullets for all of them," Travis said. "Although I'm not sure Burt would be all that happy with me using them all."

"Your father-in-law is called Burt?"

Travis smiled and nodded.

Before I could reply a bullet smashed into the window a foot above my head. "We know you're in there," Roy shouted. "Remy comes out, and anyone else gets to go about their lives."

"He's lying, isn't he?" Travis asked.

I nodded. "I've seen what they do to people they dislike. You do not want to be on the receiving end of that."

"Come on, Travis," Roy shouted again. "Or is that Burt up there. We did a little digging."

Travis' expression changed in an instant; stone cold.

"Maybe little Mary would like to come out and talk to us."

I watched the coolness on Travis' face melt, replaced with something frightening. Roy didn't know it, but I was pretty sure that was the exact moment Travis knew he was going to kill him.

Travis lowered the rifle to the windowsill, breathed in, and pulled the trigger on his exhale. The shot cracked through the glass, followed by a cry of shock from outside.

"One down," Travis whispered. "His friend wasn't expecting it though."

I peered over the windowsill as Travis fired two more shots in quick succession. Two more rounds found their homes in the heads of the witches outside.

"Down," I shouted as a roar of flame launched from one the hand of one witch, smashing into the window, showering us both with glass as the air above our heads exploded with heat for an instant before it vanished.

"So be it," Roy said. "You all die."

I fired two shots from the rifle, hitting the first two witches who stepped around the car. A third smashed into the engine, just above where Roy had crouched. I spotted a witch drawing something in chalk on the driveway beyond and put a round through the outline a few inches from his hand.

"You were aiming for the hand, right?" Travis asked.

"I can neither confirm nor deny that," I said, and crouched back behind the wall as a volley of semi-automatic fire peppered the stone building.

"They do not like you," Travis said. "Also, if more of that fire comes in and the structure collapses, Mary is in trouble. Doesn't matter how much that panic room is designed to protect her if we can't get her out again because a house collapsed onto it."

More bullets smashed into the wall followed by a second plume of fire.

"Witches use their own life force to do magic," I said. "But they've found a way to extend it using innocent victims. I think the magic is our biggest problem here."

"We need to stop them from using it on the house then," Travis said, popping up from cover and firing two more shots, before returning. "Got another one. Can't see how many are out there. Looks like a few dozen."

I picked up the Winchester. "I'm going to go outside and see if I can draw some of them away. Hopefully, my friends will arrive before they kill me. If I die, let my friends know I was super brave."

"I'll tell them you were essentially Batman."

"That works too," I said, and we shared a fist bump as I moved as fast as I was able through the room to the side door.

As I reached the rear door, a man appeared on the other side of the glass. I raised the Winchester and fired twice, the first shot taking the would-be intruder in the shoulder, and the second just under the chin as he was forced back. One less witch to worry about.

After a quick check to make sure no one was waiting for me, I moved outside, sprinting over to a set of large rocks, and moving behind them as the sounds of gunfire filled the air. Travis was only in this situation because of me. Without my appearance, he and Mary would have been living in happy ignorance of my plight ... or he'd have gone with her to the safety of the panic room.

As I came to the end of the row of rocks, a witch stood guard, facing away from me. Two shots to the back of the head, then I ducked for cover and reloaded the rifle. I counted to ten before peering around the rock again, and firing twice at the nearest witch. The first round hit him in the shoulder; the second slammed into the front grill of the large SUV he'd fallen behind.

Everyone aimed at my rock and opened fire. Pieces of stone shrapnel darted by my head, and while I was pretty sure I was safe here, I couldn't stay indefinitely.

More gunshots rang out, and the rock stopped being bombarded. The witches had taken cover from Travis, who was busy making their lives difficult. At least two of the vehicles were pretty much unusable considering the number of bullet holes in the front.

"Remy," Roy shouted. "I think you and your friend need to see this."

I peered around the corner of the battered rock. Jamal and Monique were on their knees with guns aimed at their heads.

"Travis, get away," I shouted.

"You sure?" Travis shouted back.

"Yeah, I'll deal with this."

"Come out, Remy, and your friend in the cabin gets to see his daughter again." Roy drew a dagger from the sheath on his hip. "You keep pissing me off, and I'll bathe you in their blood."

I dropped the rifle and stood, my fur-covered arms in the air. I stepped around the rock, and the rest of the witches—I counted seven in all—raised their guns my way.

Roy nodded. "Good to see," he motioned toward a female witch, and the next thing I knew I'd been hit in the chest with a beanbag round.

I tried to breathe through the pain that laced through my body. Two witches grabbed me—one under each arm—and dragged me roughly over to Jamal and Monique.

"I'm sorry," Monique said. "We thought you were in trouble and came to find you."

Roy punched her in the jaw. "Traitors don't get to talk."

He walked behind Jamal, and slit the man's throat, pushing him down onto the leaf covered earth. "They do get to bleed though."

Laughter spewed from them all and I wanted to tear his throat out as Monique cried out in anguish. Roy kicked me in the ribs before grabbing me by the throat and lifting me. "Let's see what we can do to you." He turned to the rest of the witches. "Kill them all. Make Monique watch until last."

Roy dragged me through the woods and threw me up against a log. My ribs were broken, probably my sternum too. I coughed blood, and my vision darkened at the edges. The beanbag rounds were meant to be non-lethal, but that was to a human, and when hit somewhere non-threatening. I'd taken a round from five feet away, square in the chest.

"You are going to help us," Roy said. "Louis said not to kill you, but I don't think hurting you makes much difference. You hear the gunfire? That's your friends getting closer and closer to death."

Somewhere toward the cabin, a man screamed in agony.

Roy smiled. "That didn't take long."

Something moved in the thick undergrowth behind Roy.

"You have no friends, no powers, no hope," Roy said, placing the tip of the dagger against my cheek. "You tell me what I want to know, and I'll make your death quick. Out here, alone, I won't be blamed. I'll say you ran. You keep quiet and I'll skin you."

"I do have one thing," I said, coughing up more blood.

"And what is that?" Roy asked with a smirk.

"I have a Diana."

"What the hell..." his voice trailed off as a massive hand grabbed him around the skull and lifted him into the air.

The were-bear was nearly nine feet tall and weighed more than a small car. She was covered in thick brown and black fur but didn't quite look like a normal bear standing on her back legs. Instead she was an odd mix of bear and human. The end result? A mass of horror.

Roy swiped at Diana, but she caught his arm in one massive paw, and tore the entire limb off in one swift movement. A second later, she roared into Roy's face before crushing his skull and tossing the body aside.

Diana walked up to me, and looked down before removing a key that had been on a chain around her neck. She passed it to me, and I unlocked the sorcerer's band.

My powers flood back.

I morphed into a human and passed out.

CHAPTER 7

I woke on a bed. Not the bed in the cabin but something more akin to a hospital bed. Frankly, I was getting fed up of passing out and waking up somewhere new.

Diana sat in a chair opposite the bed, the curtains behind her open to let in the sunshine. A white-faced analogue clock on the wall said it was just after ten in the morning, which meant I'd either been out for a few hours or a whole day.

"You took long enough," Diana said, smiling. She was human now, and wore a black Gun & Roses t-shirt, and a pair of dark blue jeans.

I sat and rubbed my eyes, noticing that my hands were in fact a lot closer to being paws once again. I smiled, I think I preferred being a fox-man, over just a man. The memory of what had happened the previous night abruptly ended the smile.

"Jamal?" I asked.

Diana shook her head. "I'm sorry. Mordred didn't get to him in time."

"Fuckers," I whispered. "Did everyone involved die?"

Diana nodded. "Mordred sort of lost his temper after being unable to heal Jamal. I'm pretty sure he hit them with enough power that their ancestors felt it."

"Just you and Mordred?" I asked.

"Sky came too," Diana said. "Last I saw she was talking to Travis. He came with us, by the way. Wei and Mary were busy playing poker. I think Wei was getting hustled."

"And Monique."

"She's having a hard time. Her brother was murdered in front of her. She's angry and hurt and wants vengeance. Sky and I stopped her from running off to get herself killed. I left her with Mordred."

I raised an eyebrow. "Really?"

"If there's anyone who knows what it's like to want vengeance, it's Mordred."

She had a good point. Mordred had been tortured for a century, his own brother having a hand in it. His mind had been shattered a thousand times over, and he'd been sent out to murder everyone he'd ever cared about. Then he'd died, and the horror that had been inflicted on his mind had sort of corrected itself. That's not to say he didn't have serious issues but murdering the people he loved was no longer one of them.

I dropped down off the bed and stretched. "Where are we?"

"Wei's cabin," Diana said. "She had a medical room all ready. I can't even begin to think if that's a good or bad thing."

"In the circumstances, I'm happy for it," I said. "I'm going to go see Travis, Mary, and Monique, and then I'm going to find Louis and feed him his own entrails."

"I assume you'd like company."

I nodded. "Always happy to have a friend help with feeding someone their own guts."

Diana stood and placed a hand on my shoulder. "I missed you my little fox friend."

"You too, Diana."

"Did you learn anything while you were here?"

I nodded. "A lot, it turns out."

I left the room and found Mordred perched on the large sofa. He'd somehow managed to find an old games console and set it up on the large, flat screen tv.

"I didn't even know it was here," Wei said from an armchair. Wei was difficult to spot unless she wanted you to.

"This makes me happy," Mordred said, as the kart he was

controlling on screen threw a red shell at Mario and spun him out of the race.

Mordred smiled as his kart took first place, running his hand over his bald head and sighing.

Wei picked up a second controller.

"Competition?" Mordred asked with a smile.

"Prepare to be stomped," Wei said with a grin that made Mordred laugh.

I left Diana with the two gamers and headed out to the porch. Travis sat in a chair to one side, vaping, while Sky and Mary played a game of cards on the opposite side, using a small table to put large amount of chocolate sweets they were using as currency.

"How you doing, Remy?" Travis asked me.

"Better than I've been in a while," I said. "Thanks for your help. I'm sorry it all went a bit shit."

Travis waved me away. "I phoned my wife and told her what happened. She's heading up this way to pick us up."

"She okay?" I asked.

"Mary or my wife?"

"Both," I said leaning against the wooden post beside Travis.

"Yeah," Travis said with a small smile. "Mary is just fine. Hopefully it stays that way. Weird how resilient kids are. More so than most adults I know. They just take things in their stride, but I'll keep an eye on her. A gunfight is never an easy thing to go through. I imagine it's even harder when it's your dad doing the shooting."

"And your wife?"

"Hannah asked me if I could have gotten Mary out before the shooting started, and I told her the truth. Probably not. Not without those witches coming after us thinking you were escaping. She was fine after that. She's angrier at the witches. She asked if you were okay."

"I'm good," I said.

"That's what I told her. Said it was a good job we found you or you'd probably be dead. Or very much wish you were. Those witches weren't playing. I'm sorry about that kid who died. That was done just because they could. No reason for it. No reason except because they wanted to."

I nodded. "Pretty much."

"You going after the rest of them?"

I nodded again. "They need burning out."

"I can't help you with that, I'm sorry. I need to get my daughter home."

I stared at Travis for a moment, and I knew that had been hard for him to say. To leave someone to fight without his standing by them, especially someone he'd already fought with. Must have been counter to everything he'd ever been taught.

"Go home," I said. "You did more than anyone in your position should ever be forced to do."

Travis held out a hand, which I shook. "I want to change what I said earlier, about you not being the weirdest thing I've ever seen. I think you might just be. I've seen the news, seen how Avalon are painting you and your friends, I lost people a few years back when sorcerers started killing people all over the world. A lot of innocents died, and I knew that something was wrong about it. After I saw that fight on deployment, the sorcerer came to me after and asked if I was okay. He told me that I should keep it to myself, but that not all sorcerers were evil, just like not everyone from Avalon was good. He also told me that there were more interesting things out there than an old sorcerer. You're an interesting man, Remy Roax. And a slightly terrifying one."

I laughed. "It's been a pleasure Travis. Take care of yourself."

I walked over to Mary and Sky, the latter giving me a fist bump. "Not dead yet, I see," Sky said.

Sky was the adopted daughter of Hades and Persephone. Yes, *the* Hades and Persephone. She'd been born to a Native American Chief and European Missionary who had fallen in love. Unfortunately, not everyone had been happy with their union, and both had been murdered. Even more unfortunately for those who had carried out the killings, Sky's father had worked for Hades, who hadn't taken the news well and erased everyone responsible. Sky's birth name was Mapiya, a Sioux name, but she preferred to be called Sky for her own reasons. She was a necromancer of such incredible power; I wasn't entirely sure just how powerful. Not too far off Hades, I would imagine.

"I'm being hustled," Sky said.

"Some people are just better at cards than others," Mary said with utmost innocence.

"How are you doing?" I asked Mary.

"I'm rich in chocolate," she said with a smile.

I laughed. "You okay with everything that happened?"

Mary nodded. "Bad guys turned up. Bad guys have been dealt with. That's what Daddy said."

"You're not wrong," Sky said.

"You got hurt again," Mary said to me.

"It's just a flesh wound," I said theatrically.

"What?" Mary asked.

"He's quoting a film I'm pretty sure you're not old enough to have seen," Sky said.

"I'll ask Daddy later," Mary said.

"Kiddo, I think I'm bankrupt," Sky said with a sigh. "I'm going to take Remy to see Monique."

"Okay, it's was nice cleaning you out," Mary said with a huge smile, which faded a moment later. "Tell the lady that I'm sad her brother died. Grandpa says that you go to heaven when you die, that God welcomes you into his loving embrace. Daddy always says that Grandpa is talking out of his..." she shifted slightly and pointed to her bum. "But he uses a different word that I'm not allowed to say."

"I'll tell her," I told Mary.

Sky and I walked down the steps and followed the path until we were out of earshot. "Mordred couldn't heal him," Sky said.

"I know. Diana said he lost his temper a bit after."

"Just a bit. I let Monique talk to him," Sky said. "Jamal, I mean. I absorbed his spirit and let him talk to her through me."

I stopped walking. "I didn't know you could do that."

"I don't *like* doing it," Sky said. "The newly dead are difficult. Emotional. No necromancer enjoys that, but she deserved to say her final words, and hear his. They're just kids really. Kids who came here for help, and one of them got killed."

"They came here to stop Louis," I said. "And we're going to do exactly that."

"Good," Sky said. "I'd like very much to have a long and painful chat with him and anyone helping him."

"I'm sure you'll get your chance."

"When you're done, come find us all," Sky said. "We'll head up to the base and show these fuckers exactly who they're dealing with."

I shook my head. "Hood first," I said. "I need my gear, and I need to make sure some people there are safe. I don't want them to get hurt because Louis and his gang of twatwaffles are trying to find me."

I carried on alone, and found Monique sat behind a large tree. She was flicking pieces of bark into the forest beyond.

"You found me easily enough," she said before I'd even arrived.

"The nose is working properly," I told her, tapping the side of it. "I'm sorry about Jamal."

Monique nodded. "Me too."

I sat beside her. "I feel like I'm usually the one who has the smart comments, and tells people to fuck off, but I don't much feel like being the smart mouth at the moment. I feel like raining down fire on the fuckers."

Monique turned to me. "I like that idea."

"Jamal didn't deserve to die."

"They found us at the hotel we were staying in. Took us both. Bound us, forced us into a car and drove us to a military base. On the way we were told they'd found you, and so we made a detour. They would have murdered me, and that poor girl and her father if your friends hadn't turned up. I'm not a fighter, Remy. I haven't had decades of training. I'm a scholar. I came here to ask for your help to stop a madman from murdering innocent people in a relentless need to live forever. I research. I read. Jamal too. Maybe if we'd been fighters—"

"No," I said before she could finish. "Don't do that. No amount of training would have prepared you for what happened. Any of us could get jumped and subdued. Hell, I did. Jamal didn't die because he's well read and thoughtful. He died because Roy was a fucking asshole, and Louis is an even bigger fucking asshole. And if Roy hadn't already died, I'd have taken his head and inserted it up Louis."

Monique smiled before a large sigh escaped her lips. "Our father murdered our mother. We both watched him do it. The coven had him killed for it. We watched that too. I was fourteen when it happened, Jamal nearly sixteen. He'd been in coven custody for five years at that point. They were not good years for him. He was a bully and a thug, and violent to all of us. When he died, I saw the relief that escaped from Jamal. I saw that he was at ease for the first time. I'd hoped that neither of us would see violence like that again. And then Louis happened. He needs to be stopped. Despite Jamal's death, I still have to help you stop Louis. I just don't know how."

I got to my feet. "We're going to Hood. Or I am, I'm not sure who's joining me. After that, we're going to go find Louis and end this before it gets worse for the people of this state. I don't fancy leaving Louis in a place that also has nuclear missiles."

"You think he'll go after them?" Monique asked.

I shrugged. "You want to find out?"

She shook her head.

We headed back to the cabin, where Travis and Mary said their goodbyes as Hannah had arrived. The rest of the team had joined us outside of the cabin to watch the small family drive away.

"We told them we'd take care of the damage," Mordred said. "I'm sure between us all, we know people who can help."

"Very kind of you," I said.

"Travis and Mary got thrown into the middle of something

they had no business being involved in, and stood their ground," Mordred said. "That deserves something."

"Couldn't agree more," Wei said. "We all going to Hood then?"

Diana and Sky nodded, and I turned back to Monique who also nodded.

We all climbed into one of two SUVs, Sky taking the wheel of the one I sat in, along with Monique. Diana, Mordred, and Wei took the other, and they followed us toward the town of Hood.

I saw the smoke and smelled the burning well before we arrived at the entrance to the city.

The town was aflame. Not one or two buildings, but entire streets threw flame and black smoke into the sky.

"What the hell happened?" Sky asked.

I was out the door and sprinting into the town, ignoring the multitude of bodies that littered the streets until I reached the bar.

"Son of a *bitch*," I whispered. They'd crucified Danny's body to the exterior of the bar.

Diana was the first to join me, with Wei just a short distance behind.

"You knew him?" Diana asked.

I nodded but remained silent as I walked into the bar. It had been left alone, but everyone inside was dead, maybe a dozen people. Bullet holes adorned the walls, and there was a smell of burning flesh. Magic and guns.

I ran up the stairs to my room, taking the steps two at a time, and suddenly found myself at the top of the stairs. I stopped and looked back down the staircase. Wei did say other abilities might arrive in due time. Teleportation was not one I'd considered, but I was happy to have it.

A kick to the door and I found my room ransacked. Severed heads had been placed on my bed. I didn't recognize the people, but it didn't take a genius to figure out the meaning behind it.

I pulled open the floorboards and removed the bag inside, glancing at the heads as I pulled on the black leather armor that had been rune scribed— Norse dwarven runes helped deflect magical and physical attacks. The two custom-made black-bladed short swords, still in their dual scabbards, I slung just behind my hips. My long black coat came next, my tail pointing through the slits at the back. I removed the custom-made twelve shot automatic pistol that at one point had been a Glock 26, but by the time Zamek and his people had finished with it was probably nothing like one. I placed it in the hip holster for a quick draw.

When I was done, I met Wei back outside. "The others have gone to help anyone alive."

"There's no one," I said.

"That's what Sky and I said," she told me. "I assume you're pretty angry at the moment."

"I can teleport."

"Not surprising given what you are," Wei said. "You didn't answer my question."

"I'm going to murder every single fucking one of them," I snapped. "How's that for an answer."

Wei smiled. "The one I was hoping for."

CHAPTER 8

Mordred, Diana, and Sky had found few survivors who had rounded themselves up at the town hall.

"The sheriff and his deputies helped the witches do this," Mordred told me as I waited by the SUVs outside of the town hall. I hadn't wanted to go inside in case I lost my temper, which was a very real possibility.

It was nice to be a fox-man again, I hadn't realized how much I'd missed it in the month of being human. I was pretty sure I was going to stay fox-man for the foreseeable future, unless I needed to heal or the like. I drew one of the swords out of the sheath. It had been custom made for me and would have been almost unusable in my human form. I guessed that coming here had made me realize more about myself than I'd thought.

Hood had been the scene of an horrific slaughter of over four thousand people. Maybe a quarter of the townspeople survived the witches and their murderous ways. A sigh escaped my lips, my swords were going to spill a lot of blood before I was done in North Dakota.

"What happened?" I asked.

"The witches arrived in full force last night. They started drawing marks on people's homes, and then they killed a dozen around the edge of town, and the magic burst out. I'm pretty sure a few of the witches gave their lives to power the spell." Mordred looked back at the town hall. "Never seen anything like it."

"All of these people died so Louis can make himself something special," I said. "Any ideas where he went?"

Diana and Sky walked from the building together. "Back to the military base," Diana told me. Sometimes I forgot just how good her hearing was.

Wei looked out of the window of the car beside me. Monique still sat in the back beside her; she'd had a difficult time understanding why anyone would want to murder so many people. I thought she might still be in shock from her brother's death, and hoped she'd be able to deal with whatever came next. Wei offered to keep an eye on her. I wasn't sure how good of an idea that was, but it wasn't like were swimming in good ideas.

"Some of them followed the witches out hoping to make sure they were gone," Sky said. "They executed the mayor by essentially turning his organs to liquid. It is not a pretty sight. There's a dead witch in there too. Didn't know something that powerful was part of their spell set."

"It isn't normally," Mordred said. "But apparently all bets are off."

Everyone got back into the SUVs, with Sky taking up the driving position once again, while I sat in the back with Wei and Monique.

"Are you ready for this?" I asked Monique. "Because there's no way this doesn't turn into a bloodbath."

"They deserve what's coming," Monique said.

"Yes, they do," Sky agreed. "Actually, they deserve worse but we don't have time for worse. A lot of magic is getting thrown around, and with Mordred a lot more is about to be, so let's not have Avalon descend on us because they saw something interesting."

"You think they will?" Wei asked.

"North Dakota has nukes," Sky said. "I think Avalon will want to ensure the nukes stay under the control of people loyal to them."

"Could Louis be going after the nukes?" Monique asked.

"He wants to live forever," Wei said. "Not much point in

lording that over everyone if you've turned everything into a radioactive wasteland." Wei turned to me. "You upset I told Diana where you were and gave Jamal and Monique their number to call?"

I shook my head. "Did you know about Louis?"

Wei nodded. "But not until Diana told me a few days ago. And then I didn't know the whole story and his link to you. Not until after Jamal's death and Monique told us all. If I'd have known all of it, I wouldn't have brought you here. I thought here might be good for you. There are witches, and witches usually mean—no disrespect, Monique—stupidity."

"A little disrespect," Monique said. "We're not all power-mad assholes."

"No, but the ones we've dealt with have been," Wei said.

"Good point," Sky said.

"Anyway, I figured a little stupidity might help you deal with what's happened," Wei said. "That you might be able to figure out how to get past the shitty parts to the better. Seems these particular witches were of the *holy shit, what the fuck is wrong with you?* kind."

"I did not tell Diana everything about why we were coming," Monique said. "I told her we needed your help, and that it was to do with the coven who turned you. Maybe I should have. Maybe if we'd not been so secretive, Jamal would be alive."

I looked out of the window as the car sped along an empty road, the trees either side hurtling past in a blur. "You can't think like that," I said. "It'll drive you insane with the what ifs. Trust me, I know. I've done it myself. I think we probably all have."

"More than once," Sky said without looking back at us as she took a corner a little faster than was probably necessary and needed to be immediately corrected. "Sometimes it's a hard lesson to learn that no matter what you do, bad people will always be there. They'll always do something unexpected."

"I miss Nate," I whispered with a sigh. "My friend died, and I wasn't there to help him, and that hurts. And I wasn't there to help Danny, that poor kid at that bar when those fuckers arrived.

And I know that neither of those things are my fault, but I'm still going to take it out on the only group of utter bastards that I can— Louis and his people. Why you're here, why I'm here, none of that really matters now. Just stopping them is all I want to do. And when that's done, we're going to go find Avalon and we're going to stop them too."

"Yes we are," Sky said. "For everyone they killed. For all we've lost."

The rest of the journey was a silent one until Sky pulled the SUV to a stop a few hundred meters outside the military base. We exited out and found Mordred and Diana beneath a copse of trees close to the base.

"Lots of witches," Mordred said. "A few innocent people too. They took hostages."

"And runes drawn all over," Diana said.

"I'll get inside," I said, my tale twitching with excitement as the thought of being able to let loose on Louis and his witches passed through my head. "I'll make sure the hostages are safe and then we tear everyone in half."

"Sounds like a plan," Wei said. "I'll come with you."

"Oh, look out for a silver-haired woman," I said. "I kind of forgot all about her, with everything going on, but she's a big old bag of rabid frogs crazy."

"Thank you for the warning," Mordred said. "The really, quite weirdly put, warning, but thank you nonetheless."

Crouched low, Wei and I moved toward the barbed-wire tipped fence and spotted the runes drawn on the opposite side.

"We touch the fence, something bad happens. That sound about right?" Wei said.

"I don't know what the rune does, but that would be my guess, yes."

Wei ran toward the fence, turning into smoke just before she hit it, and reappearing behind a large green tent a few feet inside the base. She looked inside and turned back to me. "Medical stuff in here. Let's go."

When I looked down at my pawtips, I felt the surge of

power. I hoped I knew what I was doing. I'd always been told by sorcerers that new powers are all about losing yourself to them. To trust your body and brain to do the thing you want it to. I'd teleported earlier without thinking about it. I hoped that would be the case again.

A deep breath, and I ran at the fence. Next thing I knew I was standing beside Wei.

"You teleported through," Wei said with a smile and pat on my shoulder. "I knew you could do it."

"I didn't."

"Just trust your instincts," she said. "These powers have been latent your entire life. All the work we've done since you got here has prepared you for this."

"You threw me off a cliff."

"And that helped prepare you," Wei said tapping me on the nose with her finger.

The guard post sat a hundred meters away from where we stood hidden. There were three guards, which was barely an issue so long as we got rid of them before they alerted everyone in the base, and the hostages were killed. I glanced inside the tent and saw a few things that might be helpful if anyone was injured.

"Hostages," I said, sniffing the air. "I don't know what I'm trying to smell here. Scents heavy with fear? There's a lot of that, it's almost overpowering."

"If in doubt go with fear," Wei said. "That building there."

I followed her pointed finger to a four-story building roughly in the middle of the base. It was where I'd been housed. Didn't exactly bring about a lot of fond memories. There were guards on the roof, and others patrolling around it. I wondered if we had time to wait until the middle of the night before we did anything, but then someone was dragged out of the building by two men. They took him to the collection of crosses set up in the courtyard and beat him with sticks until he no longer moved. Only then did they hoist him onto the cross, tying his wrists and ankles to the wood.

Wei rested a hand on my shoulder. "You're thinking of

doing something silly."

I shrugged. "I usually am, yes."

"Do you want to share your lunacy?"

I shook my head. "No, I think you'll enjoy the surprise. When we cut through those runes there's going to be a backlash that will more than certainly make everyone on the base aware of us. We need the hostages out, and preferably a way into the base without a lot of soldiers here. We don't have to get the hostages out of the base, just out of the way."

"Or seal them inside their cells and ensure no one can get to them," Wei suggested.

"That would work too." I glanced back at Wei and smiled. "I'm thinking explosion."

"I'm pretty sure that's your default state," she said.

I ignored her. "I just need to figure out *how* and *where* to actually get the explosives. It wasn't like I was given a tour the last time I was here."

"We need intel," she said, setting off before I could say anything. She turned into her fox self, and a moment later was more smoke than person. A wisp of silver and orange that you'd barely even know was there unless you were looking right at it.

I watched as the little flicker of smoke moved toward one of the guards who was patrolling closest to us. He walked behind a barracks building, and while we could see him, those at the outpost couldn't. He stopped and lit a cigarette. Technically he was in view from anyone at the crucifix, but they were so busy admiring their own handiwork, that when the mist curled around the soldier, they saw nothing. The soldier removed his glasses and cleaned them, as if the mist was dirt to be wiped away, but it continued to curl around him before it snapped shut like a hunter on its prey.

Wei appeared behind the witch, subduing him in a chokehold. She wrapped her legs around his waist and sat back, forcing him to the floor. She rolled him from her and got to her feet. Wei slung him over her shoulder and sprinted back, dropping the unconscious witch on the ground.

"And how to we get answers?" I asked.

"Like this." Wei placed her hand against the man's head, her eyes rolling up so that only the sclera showed.

"How many witches?" Wei asked.

"Thirty," the man said.

"You all ex-prisoners?"

"Some came from the other covens. Louis made them an offer they couldn't refuse."

"How many hostages?"

"Thirty. All human. They will be used to power Louis' magic. They will make us all immortal."

Wei looked back at me.

"Louis lied to them," I said. "No one is getting that power but him. Not until he's figured out how the spell works again. And he needs time and bodies to do that." I thought of something. "He needs witches, powerful witches to do the spell properly. I think that's why it's not working for him, why the lives he uses burn out so quickly. He's using humans not witches."

Wei grabbed the man's radio. "I have a plan."

"Does it involve explosions?" I asked.

Wei thought for a second, her eyes going back to normal. "Yes, actually, it does."

"I'm all for it then." I gave her the thumbs up.

Wei placed her hand back on the soldier's head. "What's your name?"

"Wesley."

"Where are the hostages?"

"Basement level of the main building."

Wei turned back to me. "When I say run, teleport back through that fence and make for the rest of the group at the trees."

"Why?" I asked.

"Because this will knock down the runes, and hopefully distract those involved long enough for me to get into that building and check on the hostages."

"And why aren't I going with you?"

"Because, and I mean this nicely, you draw attention to us,

and you really want to stab everyone here. We need those people free before you do that."

I didn't want to admit that she had a point, but she did actually have a point.

"Count to a thousand once you're at the trees and then come get me. I'll make sure I'm down there protecting the people, but you need to get through any resistance as quickly as possible. Louis sounds like he could be a problem."

"Not for long," I assured her.

Wei placed her hands back on Wesley's face, who picked up his radio and switched it on. "There's a problem with one of the runes," he said, his lips moving in time with Wei's. It never ceased to amaze me how Wei was capable of screwing with someone's head. It was genuinely terrifying and impressive.

"Wait for back up," the voice on the other end said.

I ran back to the fence, making sure to ignore the rune drawn on the ground, and teleported through the barrier to the other side, sprinting on to the tree line.

"So, do you now have a plan?" Sky asked.

"Sort of," I told her as Wei hoisted the man onto her shoulders and dumped him on top of the rune. She drew a blade from his belt and cut his hand, placing it on the rune then vanished from sight.

As the rune ignited, the fence—for fifty feet either side—was vaporized in an instant. The power surge destroyed several more runes closest to it, causing a cascade of power along the fence.

"Well," Mordred said. "That's certainly something."

"You ready?" I asked, standing upright and drawing my swords. "We count to a thousand, and then we go stop Louis."

"Time to stop some witches," Mordred said, a blade of light appearing in his hand as his glyphs blared over the backs of his hands, moving up his arms.

CHAPTER 9

Counting to a thousand felt like a lifetime, and by the time I got to nine hundred, a dozen guards had gone to investigate the death of one of their own and the chain-reaction that destroyed a large chunk of their protection.

I was already moving forward as I hit a thousand. The witches saw us sprinting toward them, and while they tried to call for help, Mordred's air magic smashed into the group, throwing them aside with ease. I teleported past one witch, and drove my sword into the heart of another, before vanishing then reappearing behind the first witch. When he turned, my sword pierced his heart.

Diana was busy tearing apart anything she could get her were-bear paws on, and Sky cut through the unprepared witches with her necromancy, plucking souls from those who had died, turning them into pure energy and throwing them back at their own comrades.

Mordred was... well, it's sometimes had to describe Mordred. He's a force of nature. Pure magical energy on a level even other sorcerers wouldn't want to fuck with. Between his air and water magics, he was a force to be reckoned with. Add his light and mind magics, the latter of which was almost purely defensive, and he was a flesh and bone tank. None of the witches even got close before a blade of light, or a spear of air destroyed them.

All twelve were dead in less than sixty seconds, although

the alarms that suddenly rang out around the base ensured more would be on their way.

"I'll go with Monique to deactivate any more runes," Sky said.

Monique had made it clear that she was not a fighter, and Sky had already suggested she stay back so as not to become an issue for anyone else. I'd seen the determination in her face to help, but Sky had a point. Monique was not a trained killer. No matter how much she wanted to help, now was not the time to decide to become something she wasn't.

"We'll fuck up everyone inside," I said. "You gonna be okay?"

Sky rolled her eyes at me. "Yes, Remy, I think I'll manage."

"I like to check," I told her. "What with you being so dainty and everything."

Sky laughed and ran off with Monique as the rest of us readied for the next wave of witches. Before they got far though, Susan arrived. The silver-haired psychopath I'd met before threw balls of fire which exploded over Sky as she wrapped herself in her necromancy, using the power as a shield, while Monique created a fog that clouded Susan's sight, although that just seemed to mean she threw more fire in all directions.

Sky reached Susan and punched her in the face hard enough that I was pretty sure she'd broken the witches' nose. The fight was short and brutal, with Sky breaking bones and letting out her anger and frustration on Susan, who clearly wasn't half as powerful as she'd believed. It ended with Sky driving one of her soul weapons—a physical manifestation of her necromancy power, in Sky's case a large scythe—into Susan's head. The witch dropped to the ground as if her strings had been cut.

Mordred started to hum a tune.

"I don't recognize that one," I said as I charged toward the eight witches who stormed out of the building. These ones were different from the last and started to fling fire magic, mostly missing us, but certainly igniting the surrounding tents.

Mordred avoided a plume of flame from one witch, by

wrapping himself in a shield of dense air. The fire died down, and the air shot out from around Mordred, forming a hundred small spikes that smashed into the witch with incredible speed, killing him instantly.

"Streets of Rage 2," Mordred said. "It's a classic."

I avoided a blade of ice, and slashed up with one of my swords, cutting off the hand of the witch who had created it. My second sword skewered her heart.

As I moved past, the head of one female witch bounced along the ground in front of me.

"Sorry," Diana shouted as she beat another witch to death with what appeared to be his own arm.

"I've always wanted to see someone do that," I said.

Diana stopped and crushed the man's head beneath her foot, dropping his arm to the ground with a wet noise that made my skin crawl. "You worry me, Remy," she called out.

I shrugged. "If it helps, it was nowhere near as entertaining in real life as it was in my head. It was kind of gross."

"I don't think that helps," Mordred said.

Judging by the expression on Diana's face, he had a point. "Wei is over in the main building."

The radio on one of the dead witches went off.

"Remy, it's Monique," she said.

I picked it up and answered it. "You okay?"

"Louis is making a break for it. Sky is dealing with some witches who did not want their runes destroyed, and I'm headed off after him. I'll keep my distance, but someone is going to need to back me up."

"You want help?" Mordred asked.

I shook my head. "I'll be on my way."

"We'll get the hostages to safety," Diana said.

"Kill everyone between here and there," I told her. "Trust me when I say they deserve it."

Mordred and Diana raced toward the main building while I ran across the base, following Monique's scent. Out of the corner of my eye, I saw Sky engaged with several witches, but she certainly had the upper hand and it didn't take her long to end their fight.

"You need a hand?" Sky shouted as I ran over. "There are still a lot of runes to get rid of," she said. "I can do it without Monique, but I'm a bit loathe to leave these things. They're unstable. They were either done in a hurry or by people who are incompetent. Possibly both."

"I'll go after Monique," I said. "You okay?"

Sky nodded. "Angry. All of this to feed one man's ego."

"He'll pay for what he's wrought," I told her, and sprinted after Monique. Her scent was easy to follow, and I was soon outside of the base's perimeter and heading toward the nearby forest.

Monique's scent intermingled with several others just as I reached the edge of the forest, and then abruptly stopped. I sniffed the air again, but there was nothing. I took another step. Stopped again. Sniffed. Something was wrong. Not just because the scent had vanished, although I'll admit that was a pretty big give away, but because I could smell something else. Magic.

Magic usually only has a scent after it's been used. Mordred smells completely different once he's started to fling magic about the place. Before, it's the scent of a normal human; afterwards it's something denser, more potent. It's an unmistakable scent, and once intermingled with Mordred's usual scent, means I can easily pick him out of a crowd.

This scent was slightly different. A dull, old scent, but one that pulsed occasionally, like someone trying to start the engine on an old car. Every now and again there was a spark before it died.

I took another step. Froze. The tree in front of me glowed a deep red. I took a step to my side, and saw the old rune drawn there in blood.

"Damn it," someone snapped from behind a nearby tree.

The man who stepped out holding a gun to Monique's head had once been the sheriff of Hood. I'd had so few dealings with him that I couldn't even recall his name, although it wasn't like it mattered much seeing how I planned on killing him for a host of transgressions.

Monique struggled, but the sheriff pressed the barrel harder to her head and she stopped.

"Found this one sneaking after Louis," the sheriff said. "Can't be having that. Louis is going to make us all immortal."

"Except he needs me to do that," I said. "And the only thing I'm going to be helping him do is bleed."

"He decided you're more trouble than you're worth," the sheriff snapped. "I'm just here to give him time—"

Monique elbowed the sheriff in the face. Off balance, he fired and she dropped to the ground as I drew my gun and pulled the trigger. The shot took him in the forehead, exploding out the back of his skull and painting the tree behind in brain matter.

I dropped to my knees beside Monique. There was a lot of blood. "Shit," I said. "You should have waited."

"He would have killed me anyway," Monique said, wincing. "Also, I'm pretty sure you're not meant to blame the victim for getting shot."

"Okay, point taken. Let me take a look."

Monique held her hand to the gunshot wound on her shoulder, the blood seeping between her fingers. I gingerly moved her hand and she made a noise, before reaching out and grabbing a large twig and sticking it between her teeth to bite down.

"Bullet hit the shoulder, looks like it went through the back and out the front, just by the clavicle. Do *not* move, just stay here and I'll get someone to help."

Monique passed me a radio and removed the stick. "It was his."

"You have light fingers," I told her with a smile.

"I've been called worse."

I clicked the button, hoping whoever picked up was a friend. "Any of you bastards feel like answering this would be good. Monique is hurt."

"Hey, Remy," Mordred said. "We're just cleaning up here. When I say we, I mean Wei and Diana. Honestly, I could have stayed at home. How bad is she?"

"Bullet hit her. She's bleeding a lot, but it looks like it went clean through. Or as clean as a bullet gets when it might have hit bone."

"I'll get Diana to bring me to her," Mordred said, his voice suddenly serious. "I failed her brother; I will not fail her again."

I passed Monique the radio. "Keep talking to them. They'll find you. Do. Not. Move."

"Yes, sir," Monique said, sarcastically.

I stripped the jacket from the sheriff and used it to prop Monique up. It was a big fluffy thing that would make sure she was a bit more comfortable. I tore his shirt off, and placed it on the exit wound, taking Monique's clammy hand and putting it over the quickly saturating shirt. "Pressure," I said.

"I know what I'm doing," she said, her voice floaty. "Hurts."

"Good, means you're not dead," I said with a smile. "Mordred and Diana will be here soon."

"Louis went that way," she said, motioning to behind me with her head.

"He can wait."

"No," Monique told me. "He can't. He needs to be stopped before he kills anyone else. He said he has a hundred souls in his body. That's a hundred times he needs to die before he stays dead."

I sighed. "That's a full-time job."

"He had his people murder my brother," Monique said, her voice as cold as ice. "He's worth it."

She had a point.

With a nod to Monique, I took off into the woods, stopping every so often for a long sniff of the air. Louis was running. Louis was scared. Louis might as well have strapped a large neon sign to his back saying *this way.*

I caught sight of the insufferable little prick as he ran toward a small hut with a large SUV parked outside. A man strode from the hut toward him. I picked up speed, teleporting when possible. While I hadn't had the ability long, it felt like second nature; I saw where I wanted to be and moved there. I wasn't sure how far I could teleport and tried to push it as far as I dared, but it seemed to be short-range only. I didn't want to push it too far, no point catching up to Louis, and then passing out from exhaustion.

Louis fumbled with something in his pocket, and eventually produced a car fob. He had one foot inside the car when I slammed into him at high speed, smashing him into the open door with enough force to shatter the window.

The second man threw me aside, blood pouring from several nasty cuts on Louis arms, and drew his gun, firing at me as I teleported around the car.

"Stay still," the man commanded, as I teleported over the car, onto the man's head, drove my sword into his throat, twisted it, and leapt off as Louis started the car and floored it, running over his dying ally.

I teleported again and managed to land in the back seat of the SUV, one of my swords drawn. Louis turned the wheel sharply, throwing me across the seat. My head hit the window, causing the glass to spider-web, and I dropped my sword in the footwell.

"You can't drive for shit, Louis," I said, as he slammed on the brakes and I hit the back of the passenger seat, falling to the footwell. I reached for the sword but it skittered into the front of the car, out of reach.

I drew my gun and fired twice into Louis' side. He slumped onto the steering wheel. The SUV lurched into speed, and I teleported out of the vehicle just before is smashed into a large tree. Unfortunately, I hadn't taken into account where I would end up when I teleported. On the plus side, the ground was fairly soft but I narrowly missed slamming headlong into a tree and had to teleport again.

With a shaky breath, I sat and took a moment. The gun was no longer in my hand, which put it either somewhere in the woods or inside the car. The latter was the most dangerous, and as the engine spewed smoke, I ran over to the vehicle.

Most of the front of the SUV was embedded in the tree, and after the initial impact, the car had spun ninety degrees, causing the rear door to smash into another tree.

I yanked on the rear passenger door, but it was stuck. When

I looked through the window, Louis was missing. "Well, that's just bollock kickingly fantastic," I said with a sigh.

Two bullets slammed into the SUV door beside my head, and I threw myself aside, teleporting behind the tree for added protection. The continuous use of my teleporting was starting to drain my energy. I had to slow it before I became exhausted. But I also had to kill Louis a hundred times over.

"You have become a nuisance," Louis shouted.

"You kidnapped me, tried to murder me, tried to murder my friends, actually murdered my friends, murdered a whole town, and you're the one who's angry? Go fuck yourself, you jumped-up bag of dicks."

Smoke poured from the SUV, and I cursed myself then teleported away before it exploded. I dropped to one knee and felt like I'd just run a marathon. No more teleporting for a while.

"You can't keep running," Louis said. "I asked for your help, and you refused. You got those people killed, not me."

He was right about the can't keep running. I grabbed a rock and threw it to my left. A ball of flame shot over to the area as Louis screamed in rage, giving me time to scramble up the side of the tree trunk and onto a branch forty feet aboveground.

I looked down on Louis, whose skin was cracking, orange power leaking out of it like magma from a volcano. He was going to kill himself using his magic, although it wasn't like he didn't have lives to spare. He carried a dagger in one hand and my gun in the other. I really liked that gun, so being shot by someone else using it would have pissed me off no end.

"Where are you?" Louis roared, throwing around more fire. He staggered back, dropped to one knee and a moment later he was back on his feet, looking as though he'd just woken up for the day.

He comes back to life quicker than I do. I dropped off the branch as he walked underneath, my sword cutting through his wrist, removing the hand. An instant before I hit the ground, I teleported several feet back. Louis screamed in pain, and I took a step forward to finish the job but it was like my legs were made of stone. Okay, so no more teleporting. Now I *really* meant it.

Louis snatched his hand from the ground, turned and ran. I retrieved my gun, and, placing it back in its holster, went after Louis, who had bled out less than a few hundred feet away and fallen down a steep bank.

I navigated the bank slowly, keeping Louis in sight the whole time, but when I reached the bottom, he was already back on his feet. His hand was healed fully.

"So, you can heal removed limbs if you die and your limb is near the body," I said. "Good to know."

Rage and hate radiated from him, crackling the surrounding air.

"You got another hundred kills in you?" he asked.

I drew both of my swords and nodded. "Yeah, I think I can manage that."

CHAPTER 10

Louis threw fireballs at me as he charged. I dodged, used a large rock as a jumping point, and drove my sword at him. He side-stepped and put more distance between us. I chased him down, but a blast of air magic sent me spiraling away, landing in a heap on a bunch of leaves.

I rolled to my feet and sprinted at Louis as he threw another ball of fire. I hoped to whatever god wanted to listen that this wouldn't kill me, and teleported behind him, my claws digging into his flesh as I ignored the surprise that it had worked, and leapt up to his shoulders before sinking my teeth into the back of his neck. My bite severed his spinal cord, bathing my muzzle with his blood.

Magic exploded from Louis' body, throwing me back. I hit the ground hard. Louis' body was already healing itself, but as I got back to my feet, the man screamed in pain. His hand was becoming translucent, the bones and blood vessels easy to see beneath the skin. Part of me knew I had a chance to kill him, but another part wanted him to suffer a bit.

"Having difficulties?" I asked.

Louis's face was a mask of agony.

I sauntered over, taking pleasure in pain and fear as I whipped the sword blade across his exposed throat then took a seat at a nearby tree.

"I can't do this all day, it will get boring really quick," I muttered. "There really does have to be a better way."

Louis stirred, and I moved fast, driving my blade into the side of his skull, before retaking my seat.

"I just don't feel very productive," I said.

Sky arrived after I'd killed Louis three times more.

"I'm getting bored," I told her.

She drew a gun and shot him in the back of the head as he began to move. When he moved for a second time, she shot him twice more. "That felt satisfying after what he's done," she said.

"I've killed him half a dozen times now," I said. "He just keeps coming back to life. How's Monique?"

"She's fine," Sky said, sitting beside me. "Hurt, but Mordred got to her in time."

Louis stirred, followed immediately by a blast of air magic that seemed to pour out of him like a shockwave. Sky and I were thrown aside, both of us rolling further down the bank, which gave Louis time to get back in his feet and turn to run.

I drew a silver blade from my hip and threw, catching him just above his hip. He dropped to his knees and tried to pull out the blade, but I was already moving. By the time he'd managed it, Louis swiped at me with my own blade, but it was clumsy and slow, and easily dodged. I thrust my sword under his arm, the blade piercing through his shoulder blade. I shoved hard, and Louis roared with pain just as Diana arrived.

"We need to stop him moving," I said.

Diana picked him up in one hand and smashed him, back first, into the nearest tree. She drew my other sword and drove it through his chest and into the tree trunk, pinning him in place.

"Like a really shit butterfly," Diana said. "How many times do we have to kill this asshole?"

"About ninety," I said.

"This is not how I hoped to spend my day," Diana said as Sky joined us.

"Won't just keeping him there cause him to wake up and die?" Sky asked.

"I think that occasionally he has a slight window of invulnerability," I said. "Enough to still use magic. Enough to still be a threat."

"So we need a more permanent solution," Sky said, thoughtful. "Bury him alive? Let the ground do the job for us?"

"Still means it's possible he'll get a chance to use one life for a massive blast of power," I said as Louis finally died.

"I have an idea," Wei said as she appeared with Monique and Mordred. "It's probably not very nice."

Louis stirred again, and Wei dropped a leather satchel on the ground, removed my sword from his chest, and used it to decapitate Louis in one quick motion. Wei passed the sword back to me, and picked up Louis' head, carrying it ten feet away before dropping it at the foot of a tree.

Louis woke. Louis tried to scream. Louis died.

"Wow, that's really horrible," Mordred said as Louis' body convulsed, and his head woke up for a second time. A second time of trying to scream, but no sound emerged. A second time of dying.

"I get the feeling this could take a while," I said.

"We'll go finish cleaning up at the military camp," Sky said. "I do not want to watch a head die a hundred times."

"I'll stay with you," Wei said to me, taking a seat at my side.

Diana and Mordred also left, with Monique deciding to stay behind too.

"I want to see it," she said. "The last life leave his body."

"I can understand that," I said.

"I'm sorry you lost your brother," Wei said. "I know what it's like to lose people you love."

Monique nodded and sat on the ground. "So, we're almost done here."

"Witches defeated, everyone who needed killing is dead," I said. "It took a lot of life lost to do it through. A lot of pointless deaths to feed one man's ego."

Wei opened the satchel and removed dozens of pieces of paper. "This is what I found that belongs to Louis," she said as Louis died again. "Some woman had them. She did not want to give them over. It took some convincing."

"Is she dead?" I asked, remembering that she'd been there when Louis had his people torture me.

"Yes," Wei said. "She's very dead. These are Louis' notes about how you came to be. About how he could absorb life. They're incomplete though."

I took the notes and started to read through them. "He had his memories of when he performed the spell wiped. He wanted to know how I had survived the spell. But he knew as he'd made himself powerful in a similar way, so I was confused as to why he'd needed me." I removed the page I was looking for. "I figured there would be more to it than him just forgetting the spell, but I thought that he needed witches, or some other powerful creature, to perform it correctly and make the immortality stick. I thought that his use of humans was why he couldn't make it work properly. I was wrong."

I passed the page to Monique. "His original spell wasn't perfect," I said. "It didn't grant him immortality; it turned him into basically a vampire. He needed a constant stream of new victims. That's why he killed so many. The spell was mastered early, but it was the wrong kind of spell. He needed something more permanent, which meant me. The only thing he couldn't figure out was how I could turn human. He didn't want to be left in the body of a badger or something for the next few centuries."

"He thought that you turning into an animal was part of what went wrong," Wei said. "But he refused to entertain the idea that he'd have to sully himself by not being human-shaped. The fact that you could turn human again was what he was interested in."

"He killed the town looking for you," Monique said, reading the other pages in the satchel. "He wanted your blood; you weren't there, so he executed everyone. He wrote about it. He bragged about it. He was angry you'd killed his..." she flipped to the next page. "Roy was someone he hired to help achieve that aim, and someone who grew more and more lost in power as he saw what magic can do. That monster murdered my brother, he deserved what he got."

I walked over to Louis' head and picked it up. "However shit this is," I said to the newly revived Louis. "You deserve worse." I threw the head to Wei. "Put it in the satchel, we're leaving."

We returned to the military base without a word. Louis had murdered so many and hurt so many more just because he wanted something he couldn't have. He wanted immortality on his terms, and he was willing to kill everyone to get it. Technically, he had it now. Left alone, he'd live centuries, but he didn't want that. He wanted more power too. He wanted what I had, no matter how strange that sounded to me.

Sky, Diana, and Mordred sat outside the base, which was currently on fire. Wei removed the head from the satchel, and I took it from her, before looking over at Monique. "No one else dies because of this asshole," I said.

Something exploded deep inside one of the buildings.

"Diana, could you launch it to there from here?" I asked.

Diana threw it the several hundred feet as easily as throwing a tennis ball. Louis' head landed in the inferno. He wasn't coming back. Not from that.

Monique dropped her face to her hands and began to sob. Diana placed an arm around her shoulder to comfort her, leading her to the cars. It was time to head back to Wei's cabin. It was a drive done in silence, and when we reached the cabin, I walked off to spend a few minutes alone to think about everything that had happened.

When I returned to the cabin the everyone except, Sky and Wei had moved inside. I sat next to them on the porch, looking out across the expanse of peaceful nature before us.

"Not quite the time I had in mind," Wei said.

"Nor me," I told her.

"I think I'm going to go lose myself for a while," she said. "Being around people makes me nervous, and honestly, your lives seem like one big fight after another. It's exhausting."

"Try living it," Sky said.

"Thank you," I said to Wei, who nodded. "Thanks for your help," I said again. "Even the mountain pushing thing."

"I'll see you around, Remy." She ran into the forest, turning into a fox mid-step, and vanished from view.

"You okay?" Sky asked.

"No," I said. "But I will be."

Mordred and Diana came out, Mordred carrying a bottle of vodka while Diana held four glasses, Mordred poured a measure into each and passed a glass to the four of us.

"To everyone we couldn't save," Mordred said, raising his glass.

Sky, Diana, and I joined him in his toast, and we knocked back the vodka.

I poured everyone another measure. "To Nate," I said, raising my own glass.

Everyone nodded solemnly. "To Nate," they said in unison.

Mordred looked down at the glass in his hand, before getting to his feet and walking away.

"It'll get better," Diana said.

"I know," I told her and looked up at the clear night sky. "I know."

We sat there for several hours, until Mordred returned and Monique joined us, and we raised toast after toast to everyone we loved, and everyone we couldn't save.

The next day we packed up and drove Monique to the airport. She had no luggage as everything she owned had been destroyed in Hood's fires. I sat in the back of the SUV with her, and she hugged me. Mordred had put in a few calls and gotten her a fake Passport and cash; it would be enough to get her back to France.

"I'm sorry this didn't work out so well for you," I said. We'd burned the notes at the cabin, the last thing anyone wanted was someone trying to recreate Louis' plan.

Monique nodded. "I will not forget you, Remy. I am sorry you had to go through all this."

"Take care," I said.

She nodded and left the SUV, disappearing into the airport a few seconds later.

"You okay?" Diana asked.

I nodded. "Been a shit few days."

"We still have to deal with Arthur and Avalon," Mordred said. He looked at me. "Okay, you wanted good news. I get that."

"I took time away to deal with Nate's death and all the shit we went through, and honestly, I'm not sure I should have bothered," I said. "But I'm ready to deal with Avalon. I'm ready to do what's needed to stop them. And I'm ready to move on from losing Nate. So, maybe it did help. Who the fuck knows at this point."

"You're a complex foxman," Sky said with a smile.

"And handsome," I said. "Don't forget that."

"So, where to now?" Mordred asked.

"Greenland," Diana said. "We need to prepare for what comes next. Whatever that is."

I stared out the window as we drove toward an old airfield that was just out of town. "Thank you all," I said.

"We couldn't let you die," Diana said.

"Well, we could," Sky said with a sly smile. "But only the once."

I chuckled. "You're just jealous you don't get fur as nice as mine."

"Hey," Diana said. "My fur is beautiful, thank you very much."

"That's what it is," Sky admitted. "I wish I was furry too."

"I don't," Mordred said.

I smiled. My friends were okay, and we were going to fight oppression head on. Those fuckers didn't stand a chance.

ACKNOWLEDGE-MENTS

Novellas take just as much work as novels to get together, even if the word count is much lower, so I just want to thank everyone who helped make this novella a reality.

My wife and three daughters are, as always, one of my reasons for writing. The fact that my wife wanted a Remy novella just as badly as everyone else is probably one of the reasons I ended up writing it.

To my agent Paul Lucas, for answering any questions I had, and for being supportive of my idea to self-publish this novella. I'm lucky to have such an awesome agent.

To my publisher 47North, who when I asked if it was okay that I self-publish my novella, they were completely supportive and happy for me to do so.

To Amanda J Spedding, my editor, who was recommended to me by a friend, and I'm so glad she was. Amanda is a big part of why this novella is something I was happy to put out, she helped turn my ramble of words into a full story and for that I will always be thankful.

A massive thank you to Pen Astridge who did a frankly incredible job with the cover for Hunted. An absolute pleasure to work with, and someone who fantastically talented.

And last, but by no means least, to everyone who helped

support me over the years by buying my books and leaving reviews, or by contacting me to tell me that you loved something I'd written, thank you. Your support means the world to me.

If you enjoyed Hunted, here's the beginning of Infamous Reign, another novella set within the same world that is currently available to purchase, alongside the Hellequin Chronicles, Avalon Chronicles, and upcoming Rebellion Chronicles.

In late 15th century England, two young princes are given over by Merlin to the protection of their uncle, King Richard III. They soon vanish from sight, igniting tales of their demise at Richard's hand and breeding unrest throughout the land.

Nathanial Garrett, also known as Hellequin, is sent to London to decipher fact from rumor and uncovers a plot to replace the king. But his investigation quickly becomes personal when he learns that an old nemesis is involved. He soon finds himself racing against time to rescue the boys before their fate, and the fate of all England, is sealed in blood.

Infamous Reign is a novella in the Bestselling Hellequin Chronicles series, mixing gritty and action-packed historical fantasy with ancient mythology.

CHAPTER 1

September 1483, Tower of London.

It's surprisingly easy to gain access to a king when many of his most trusted servants and advisers also work for you.

The king's guard all moved aside, most ensuring they didn't make eye contact. Those who knew who I was also had a pretty good idea of why I was there, and so avoided me for that reason. Those who didn't know me must have sensed my dark mood and decided that pissing me off further than I already seemed to be wouldn't have enhanced their chances for a quiet life.

Thus unencumbered, I made my way through the courtyard of the royal palace toward the Grand Hall, where the king was holding court. I reached the doors and opened them, stepping through into a room that lived up to its name.

The hall was both massive and opulent, with the king's banners showing the House of York's white rose, alongside the usual imagery of fleur-de-lis and inaccurate looking griffins draped next to stunning stained-glass windows, some of which depicted the king's personal badge, a white boar.

Several dozen men and women, of all ages and ranks, stood before King Richard III of England as he sat on his throne. Each subject was given the opportunity, in turn, to ask or beg the king for whatever favor he or she wished. Some wishes were granted, some were not, it was wholly dependent on the king's mood of the day and how much he either liked or needed the petitioner. The king's judgment was final, too. Sometimes you got a good king, a just king, a king who would help his people. And sometimes you got a blood-thirsty savage. Either way, so long as Merlin and Avalon were happy, we didn't intervene in human politics. Unfortunately, on this day, Merlin was far from happy. Which led to the reason why I was here.

I resisted the temptation to make a point by removing anyone but the king from the room. He was finishing up a proclamation that permitted one of his subjects to marry someone else, and I allowed the moment to continue. It wasn't them I was angry with.

When the king finished, he noticed me for the first time, and all color drained from his face. If you're the ruler of a country and I'm standing before you, it's usually not because you're doing a good job. The first time it happens is just after a coronation. I, or someone just like me, arrives and tells you exactly where you stand in the world and explains that you either behave, which means doing the things we ask, or you'll receive another, less pleasant, visit.

The king before me knew exactly why I was there. Two princes, Edward and Richard, had vanished after being placed in his custody. He was either personally involved in something very bad, or he knew who was. It had been left for me to either fix it or to ensure that it was King Richard III's final error.

King Richard signaled to one of his aides who then told everyone that court was over and would reconvene on the morrow. I stood still as the confused masses were ushered from the hall, until only the king and I were left.

"I know why you're here," he said.

"That should make this go a lot quicker then," I snapped and walked toward him. "Your majesty." I didn't bow or even nod in his direction. That wasn't a judgment against the man; there wasn't a human king or queen alive that I would have done it for. None of them were my king.

"Hellequin, you have to understand." Fear broke through

his voice.

I stopped walking and ignited a ball of fire in the palm of my hand, making it turn slowly. "Make me understand, Richard," I said softly. "Make me realize why you disobeyed an order from Merlin."

30041589R00061

Printed in Great
Britain
by Amazon